ROUTE 28

Also by Ward Greene
Cora Potts
Ride the Nightmare
Weep No More
Death in the Deep South

ROUTE 28

WARD GREENE

CUTTING EDGE

ISBN-13: 978-1-957868-61-5

Published by
Cutting Edge Books
PO Box 8212
Calabasas, CA 91372
www.cuttingedgebooks.com

CONTENTS

CHAPTER ONE
WEST OF THE HUDSON

O N THE MORNING of this July Fourth, in a field of long grass and daisies about halfway between New York and Philadelphia in the state of New Jersey, a man named John Faith woke to the sun striking reflecting metal through the dusty windshield of his car. He was cramped in the back of the car, not a comfortable haven, for he was tall and must choose under these circumstances to be a jackknife or repose with his feet through a window. Habit had conditioned him to both methods but never reconciled him to either. He woke to pain through most of his body and cursed himself for the repetition of an old folly. The pain would go away as the day advanced beyond the first drink; his chagrin would stick, not rankling but, like the secretions of a mollusk, forming another layer in the hard, dull lump that seemed to him, in these later years, to have taken the place of his heart.

"I suppose, Jack," he said aloud, indulging another habit he had come to rely on in moments of dejection, "I suppose when you die and bequeath your worthless body to science and they cut you open they will find a pearl, and for the first time the world will profit from you. Faith, the Man-oyster! Much finer than Billy the Oysterman. But what a pity they can't operate at once; you could pay your debts."

But because the sound of his own voice reminded him of the number of people he must have bored the night before, he shook the kinks from his muscles and some from his suit and shambled out among the daisies.

He walked around the car appraising the fender dents. No new ones. He had not, then, hit anybody. He wound and tapped his wrist watch without result and considered it disconsolately. Neither, he was sure, had he socked anybody, though there had been arguments. Argument pleased him. But though Harvey Slope, being undersized, might sock, Faith never socked save in Slope's behalf and was known, in most barrooms between Bound Brook and Bucks County, as a peaceful if disputatious man. The problem of the time he settled now with a squint at the sun. No farmer, he often confounded farmers by being right when they were wrong. It was, he estimated, a quarter after eight, high time he went about his business.

He studied the landscape. Of the several fields he might have selected the night before when the zigzag behavior of the highway convinced him that home was a bad risk, this one, he recognized, was on the far side of the county in the Mastick tract. He could have quoted from the court records. But the important matter of the moment was not titles but water. The brook was there and, just below the willows, it ran deep before it joined the Raritan.

Faith bathed in the cold brook. His head began to feel better. Back at the car, he extracted from the trunk a comb and a clean shirt. The rest of him would have to do. He was a fair man and not till afternoon would bristles show on his chin, gray strays among the blond. By then most of his appointments, with any luck, would have been met.

He reviewed them with apathy mounting to distaste. Some of them he knew of old : third-and fourth-nibblers trying to make up their minds; others he would greet for the first time, covertly analyze them, make swift judgment, placate them or jolly them or needle them a little according to their kind and leave them, usually still undecided, with disgust strong in his nostrils and not all of it for them. Once the people, not the sale, had been unalloyed relish; today he did not give a damn for either.

He saw them darkling out from the city toward the Hunterdon Hills, today's flight and yesterday's and tomorrow's, like a host of locusts dropping from the skies to burrow and breed for seven years of safety. He saw them in all their variety of character and condition, from the affluent, thinking in thousands of dollars and hundreds of acres, to the scrimpers, avid for a patch of any sort to insure their savings. Once he had seen them all as dreamers and almost loved them, man dreaming his oldest dream of his own fireside and coming home to it at last as he himself had come, sore and hungry for appeasement, ten years before, through the tunnel, over the Skyway, out of the cities and the suburbs to the broad, flat lands of pasturage and dairy farms and growing grain, and past these until the road rose and dipped and rose again to the divide and below, the Valley, checkered by the streams that were flowing east to the Raritan and west to swell the Delaware. The Valley was beautiful. But these others who came afterward, who were coming today and would come tomorrow, he no longer saw as dreamers. He saw them frightened. Behind them, lowering in the east, grew a cloud that threatened their cloudless sky and they ran from it like rabbits, feeling the rock shake on which they had staked their greeds and pleasures. They ran to the country as people run to bombproof shelters, not for love but in panic, and even in the running they were mercenary, hunting bargains, counting profits, city gamblers still. If there were but one among them—one!—who came with the land an ache in his heart and stayed to cherish it, he would, had it been in his power, have deeded him the whole Valley.

"Jack," he said aloud again, "apparently you have a hell of a hangover. It must be that. You are really not old and friendless and impotent. True you are broke, but that is nothing new and if you buck up, your commissions today may keep you in whisky for a year. Go out and sell these bastards farms!"

With that, being a sucker for poetry, he recited some, especially that part of the Book of Ecclesiastes which says,

"Whatsoever thy hand findeth to do, do it with thy might, for there is no work, nor device, nor knowledge, nor wisdom in the grave whither thou goest," and, having discovered an ounce of gas still in his tank and the starter alive after four tries, he backed roadward with regret for the daisies crushed in his passage.

2

Trimble took his vacation in July that year. In other years he had chosen the vacation seasons of the wealthy. Trimble was not wealthy. But even a second vice-president, if he is alone in the world and lives prudently for eleven months, can afford to play the epicure in the twelfth. So Trimble, who hated crowds, though he could be fascinated by the sorriest individual among them, shunned the swarm and reek of summer holidays to follow the more fortunate tenth—south to Florida in December, east to Italy, on cruise boats around the Caribbees, as far west as California and the Islands. He was a pleasant fellow traveler, suave and affable and informed. Yet always he seemed on the fringe; the friendships he made were fading scarcely before the ships docked; he became accustomed to looking back at them as at so many faces in a newsreel not run twice. Each year he returned to the office a little grayer, a little less communicative, as if he harbored a secret contempt for his associates, though perhaps he but brooded on his next argosy eleven months hence. He was a lonely man, chasing a fugitive thing he could never touch, doubtful that he would recognize it if he caught it...until the afternoon he saw the house on the Barrens.

Often afterward he was to think of that day in April as anticlimax. For him had been New York, London, Cairo—the ports of strange countries, the peaks of history. And out of them he rode along a macadam highway, Mike's Bar-B-Q to the rear, the Burma Shave signs ahead, into a dirt road scarred by rains and past milk pails and a red silo to the end of a lane where undergrowth flicked the car like detaining hands. The house cowered behind weeds. Abandoned orchards hemmed it. As John Faith unlocked the rickety door Trimble kicked a child's marble, buried and weather beaten, in the path. He thought: this is a horrible bore. Yet even in the flick of his toe across the turf he sensed for an instant a vanished enchantment. Once, of earth like that, he had known its intimate way. Where the root grew. Where the rock took hold. A boy's marble had been part, then, of a world closer to the heart than any horizons. "It's a nice view from here," said John Faith.

When Trimble, returning to the Duncans' place, told them he had bought a farm they were surprisingly unsurprised. A guest arrives for a week end; John Faith takes him out; John Faith's business is selling farms; the guest buys a farm; so what? You'll not regret it, they assured Trimble in their arrogance of landed proprietors for two years. They went on calmly talking about spring planting. But then the Duncans didn't know Trimble very well; they had met him the year before in Bermuda and were not quite sure whether he dealt in rice or ryes.

Trimble's older acquaintances, in the office and the club and the East Fifties, stared their frank amazement. A farm? Are you going to be a farmer? No, I just liked it. But what will you do with it? I'll go out week ends; maybe someday I'll live there. But you can't drive a car, can you? How will you get there? And why New Jersey? Why not Long Island? Why not Westchester? Why not Connecticut? Why a farm anywhere?

Trimble himself was a little perplexed. He could say, and did, that he was buying a car and would learn to drive. He said that New Jersey farms were cheaper. He protested that they knew not New Jersey who knew only her shores, her marshes, her mosquitoes, her cities and her politicians. He talked about the view when you had crossed the Valley and climbed the far hills and looked back from the Barrens at wood and field and sky and, on clear nights, a thin flicker of lights to show the road you came by to this, the end of things.

There was nothing like it within three hours' drive of New York, said Trimble; there was nothing like it closer than Virginia. Indeed, said his friends; how lovely, they said; how interesting. Trimble felt a little silly. He felt helpless to make them understand. He felt his perplexity returning.

And all through the remainder of that month, when he was still but the owner of a deed, when he was hiring men to clear the rubble and repair the house, when he was discovering in each task accomplished a new problem to overcome, when he began to realize his personal deficiencies, such as his inability to replace a blown fuse or operate a ratchet screw driver, and particularly at those moments when, with a licensed driver at his side, he charged the new car at the trucks of West Street, yanking desperately at the gears, then did his wonder and disgust swell that he who had spent his life escaping on magic carpets the slightest threat to his freedom should be bound thenceforth to a farm.

For he could not explain to himself, and certainly not to others, that a marble buried in a patch of earth can affect the spirit as a nightingale the heart of Ruth amid the alien corn. He would forget the marble. But the glow it had kindled would smolder under all exasperations. And on a Saturday in June, when Trimble, waiting until the last workman took his Ford sputtering into the twilight, turned from the Valley's haze to the white fence and the green lawn and the house getting a little ghostly against the orchards despite its insulated roof and its brave coat of paint, the slow warmth surged in him. Shadows ran out from the apple trees, drawing the new shrubs into the old fields. But Trimble stepped past them as if he nodded to a friend. His path received his feet. Inside, where the colored man prepared supper, a lamp bloomed suddenly.

Tonight and tomorrow, thought Trimble—and in July a month.

3

He drove to the farm the day before the Fourth and at dusk, watching the lights in the Valley settle into a golden mottled serpent of unending length, congratulated himself on being well out of the muddle. Cold crept down the Barrens and Trimble went to bed under blankets. The sun rose in quiet mists and he woke to the caw of crows, smiling to think how he would have snored through taxi horns. He made coffee in the freshly immaculate kitchen before sounds beyond the wall indicated that Laurence was responsive to aroma if not to bird song, and he was drinking his second cup, stretched on the lawn in a deck chair, listening to the cicadas and the jays, when the slap of chains and the creak of harness caused him to sit up and frown.

It was odd how, through all the natural chorus that could make a hundred acres of neglected hillside as noisy as a jungle, the presence of man struck so unmistakable and harsh. Like the old missionary hymn. Where every prospect pleaseth and only... But that would be the Purdy horses coming up the lane. In the satisfaction of absolute possession he had forgotten acting on John Faith's advice that he rent the Purdys the upper fields.

Joe Purdy followed his team out of the lane. The lane was no more than a wagon track where the horses brushed sumac on either side and stumbled a little on the uncleared rocks, and the dogs that followed Joe Purdy nosed as they went for rabbits and woodchucks so that only their tails lifted above the daisies and the dogs were a mere shaking in the tall grass. Behind his team Joe Purdy walked, his stride untroubled by rocks or growth.

Trimble, seeing him for the third time, felt as sharply as ever Joe Purdy's singularity. Here was no farmer boy, gangling and sallow and snaggle toothed. His muscles were a man's in a baby's skin. His back shamed the poplars. His teeth broke the ruddy face like white pebbles on the shore of a sea no bluer than his eyes. He belongs in buff and crimson on the October number of a magazine, Trimble thought, not down there at the foot of the hill among chickens, barns and cowdung.

He got up and said "Hello, Joe"—a salute not so much to a neighbor as to the halfback of his fancy.

"Hello, Mr Trimble," said Joe Purdy. He checked the horses with a pull of the reins and stood at ease outside the white gate while the two dogs came out of the brush and stood behind him, their tongues panting and their hounds' eyes appraising Trimble where he leaned on the pickets.

"You're on the job early, Joe."

"I was up at four, Mr Trimble."

"No holiday today?"

"Not for us, sir."

He smiled again and for a moment, to Trimble, all the sun in the Valley shimmered into a single blinding jet.

"Come in," he said impulsively, "come in and have some breakfast."

"No, thanks, Mr Trimble."

"Not even coffee?"

"No, thanks. I gotta cultivate the lower field."

Trimble smiled back, the well-tailored smile of the host and older man making the shyer, younger at home, and the dogs began a slow wave of friendly tails, and bees hummed in the lilacs, and somewhere an oriole whistled above the cicadas and Trimble suddenly wished very much that Joe Purdy would come in. He thought of the thousand voices of his neighbors for a day or a week on boats and piazzas in far places and of how hungrily, patiently he had listened to them. And he thought of the thousand questions he would like to put to Joe Purdy, the personal and impersonal feeding alike that insatiable urge in him to cut the individual from the crowd.

He said, "How's your father, Joe?"

"He's all right, sir."

"And your mother?"

"She's fine."

"Fields doing all right?"

"Doin' all right, I guess."

Good Lord, he was not interested in the fields!... How do you live, Joe Purdy, down there among the barns and cowdung and ammoniac zephyrs that offend me whenever I pass your place? What do you do besides this labor that begins at sunup and flogs you choring into the night? Fighting growth to get growth; fighting drought and storm; reaping, storing, mending, guarding; priming the machine; draining the udder—we know about that; oh, we know about that; they have told us interminably since Cain, the first tiller... but what else, what lucubrations, what passions, what dreams beset you? You are a farmer boy in Sears, Roebuck overalls, by tradition as splendid as wheat or as droll as an outhouse, but you are a halfback, too, and for all I know a Buchmanite or a Red or a jitterbug, for progress has doubled upon the pioneer, its wheels and airwaves have flowed over you, leaving you dry on your hummock yet drenched to the core with its substance, and you are no longer the land's but the road's and the air's and the world's, and so what do you think, Joe Purdy? What do you do? How do you live?

He said, "Do you ever read, Joe?"

"Sure—but mostly in the wintertime. Don't get much chance the rest of the year. Keep us too busy. In winter I read in bed by the flashlight."

"Flashlight?"

"Yes, sir. Put it and the book under the covers. Too cold to stick your head out."

A flashlight under the covers! Lincoln and Blackstone by a pine-knot fire! This was still America!

Trimble said, "What do you read, boy?"

"Mostly *True Detective*," said Joe Purdy. "I like stuff with a lot of shootin' in it."

Trimble went back to the deck chair. He closed his eyes and kept them closed until the clink of trace chains died into the insect symphony and Laurence called him to breakfast. In a bright alcove of the living room, eating with relish the strawberries he had brought from New York and the imported English biscuits, he glanced once at the old contents of his new shelves. Juiced from those first editions, fresh saliva joined indignantly the excellent contents of his stomach.

"Laurence," he called out when he had lit his cigar, "if any more of the natives come around while I'm in the village, tell them I don't want to hire any help, or build any swimming pools, or buy any lightning rods—or rent any more fields."

4

The railroad, twisting out of Copperhead Gap, vanished almost immediately behind Toy Mountain, as if it ran in fear from its glimpse of the Valley. Where it bent in its crossing, Little Salem hugged the tracks like a part of the equipment left behind and striving futilely to follow the last whistle; a lost, sad little town, betrayed by the main highway which declined even to skirt it, betrayed by the railroad itself since only vagrant freights paused here nowadays on their way from there to yonder; a town without a courthouse or a post office or a public building of any kind; one church, one store, one tumble-down factory, one filling station, one gas pump pointing starkly along the macadam to the concrete a quarter of a mile away.

They had told Trimble of Little Salem's days of glory, of the boxcars by the score waiting to be loaded, of the freight sheds bulging with produce while the wagons rolled in from the farms with more and yet more, peaches, apples, cherries, tomatoes, potatoes, grain in constant harvests to meet the demand of the distant cities that seemed forever certain to look to Little Salem for their sustenance. Little Salem was to be such a city one day, they believed, and when the canning factory came they were sure of it; Industry lay with Ceres, begetting Metropolis for the time ahead. But something happened, and what it was, they who spoke with Trimble, the remembering old men who looked out from frayed lashes at the sumac swallowing their furrows, what it was, they could not say, only that suddenly, or so it seemed, the demand ceased, the freight trains dwindled, the vegetables rotted in the sheds for want of buyers and the fruit on the trees for no profit in the picking and all the years were lean years. It was like the extinction of the passenger pigeons, clouding the firmament one sunset and no single survivor in the day's dawn.

Little Salem survived but with a permanent malady. Its last house to be built at the beginning of the century was still its last-built house forty years later. When a house burned, the people moved nearer the highway and the chain stores of Madison. When the factory went for taxes a lumber company tore it down to the foundations. Progress in Little Salem came to mean a paint job on the Ford.

Trimble approved his isolation from the village, his farm as far from it on one side as the concrete was on the other. His approach, after he left his own lane and the Purdy silo, led him through deep woods obscuring all but the bumpy road ahead. Suddenly he would come off the ruts and thank-you-marms onto smooth macadam, the shadows would evaporate into sun glare and, before he had shifted gears, he was in Little Salem. A jigger of windows, an old man on a porch, a syringa bush in bloom, the church, the store, the tracks, and he was past it, always with a shake of relief, yet with a kind of qualm, too, as if he had brushed too rudely past the sleeve of a beggar.

Today, however, he did not speed up at the edge of the woods. He had made a resolution. When in Rome, trade with the Romans; be the good neighbor; patronize home industries.

He parked in front of the church. As he did so he was conscious of a radio blaring somewhere. Then it was cut off, as suddenly as his ignition.

In the July noon Little Salem might have been some desert ghost town. Ahead of him a little girl crossed the street, and the bang of the screen door, where she disappeared with a swirl of skirts, left a silence like a thunderclap's. He followed her, sensible of the crunch of his own shoes, and he entered the store feeling absurdly like an intruder. The transition from full day to dusk halted him, blinking. It was several moments before, against the drawn shutters, he could make out, instead of the cracker barrels spattered with tobacco juice which he had expected, an interior not unlike the average A & P's. Well, it was gratifying to be surprised by one's favorite brand of cereal. He inspected the shelves and counters while the child concluded her shopping, for the most poisonous pink candy, he observed, to be found outside Italy. After a pale and challenging scrutiny she went out with the same bang of the screen and her furious, conscious swirl. But Trimble had already turned to the man.

"How do you do?" he said. "Have you fresh strawberries?"

The man shook his head. He said nothing; he simply shook his head in a gesture so indifferent, so empty of regret or chagrin or even surprise, in a negation so close to complete inanimation, that Trimble repeated the question. After a pause protracted to the insufferable, without shaking his head again, without looking at Trimble, almost without moving his lips, the man said in a voice as flat as a tap's drip, "We got bananas and apples; no fresh things."

Trimble wanted to retort, Look here, a customer's not a trespasser, you know. But he bought half a dozen bananas, flour, sugar, canned peas. He bought in monosyllables and the man served him in monosyllables, seeming deliberately to move in the dim light with a minimum of sound, of effort, of expression from the counter to the shelves, across the room, back to the counter, sliding flatly along the plank floor, his bare arms hanging flat from the undershirt save when he must call on them, his hair flat to his forehead in a black and pasty fringe, his ears flat back like a mean mule's, he at last, the paper bags filled on the counter and the sum of the purchases stoopingly figured, straightening abruptly and standing flat to the shelves behind him like a man before a firing squad, and even then never once yielding Trimble so much as a squint from his averted, lashed eyes.

Trimble laid a bill on the counter and a voice somewhere said, "Emil."

The voice said again, the inflection rising, "Emil?" and Trimble, pushing money toward the man who made no motion to take it, looked up and saw his eyes open, as fixed as a cataleptic's, the pupils darkly gaping like two fathomless holes, and in them such suspense that Trimble's own eyes widened and involuntarily shot where the other's stuck, to the curtain, to the woman who in a moment parted it and stood there quietly, staring at them both, with nothing extraordinary about her, not her figure nor her starched blue dress nor her impassive face under the neatly coiled hair, yet discharging in her dark gaze (or whatever the medium was that emanated from her like chill from an iceberg) a force that abashed Trimble and shocked him, as if in that second before his eyes escaped hers he had been judged, scorned, derided, stripped and, possibly, violated a little before she flung him back to her husband.

For he supposed this was her husband, this Emil, though neither while the man handed him his change nor while Trimble was bundling the bags into his arms, crossing the store self-consciously—to fumble with his foot, because he must help himself, at the screen—neither when he had kicked it open nor when he turned in the open door did the man or woman speak to him or to each other.

He said, out of sheer nervousness, "I'm Trimble—bought the old Heinschmidt place, you know."

The woman no longer stared. Her eyes had traveled to the ceiling where a fly circled among the sticky suspended coils.

"Yes," said the man, "yes—we know."

The woman watched the fly. Trimble had seen bird dogs point; flushing, he closed the screen.

Not until he was halfway home did he stop fuming. That two rude yokels should upset him was, he told himself, a commentary on his own lack of poise and common sense. They probably weren't even rude, merely reticent. And why shouldn't they freeze up when city strangers barged into their solitude grinning fond expectation of welcome? He himself resented invasion of his farm and, for that matter, hated effusive clerks in town. The store, he supposed, was the man's and woman's home too. They'd been been natural; he was the sensitive ass.

Yet, bumping out of the woods again, he could not lose entirely his feeling of the interloper. Ahead of him he saw the child who had been in the store, seated on a grass bank at the side of the road, devouring, he presumed, her unwholesome treasure. He passed her without a glance—and reproached himself immediately for not waving. When Mrs Purdy hailed him where the road met the lane he pulled up almost gratefully.

5

Mrs Purdy, at least, could talk; indeed, talk to her was like whisky to a drunkard. She abandoned whatever she was doing, wiped her hands on her apron, waddled the three steps from her kitchen to the old hitching post, pillowed her arms on it and beamed like a fat and amiable billiken.

"Mr Trimble!—It's good to see you—I said to Lance this morning, 'I bet Mr Trimble's here'—heard a car pass yesterday while I was out back—just about four o'clock, wasn't it?—'I bet he's come out a'ready for the long holiday,' I said, and I told Joe to be sure and tell you when he went up with the team—'Joe,' I said, 'be sure and tell Mr Trimble to stop, I must give him some of my green tomato mincemeat'—just two jars left—I bet that recipe's been in my family more 'n a hundred years——"

Trimble marveled at the fate that condemned such a woman to an audience of hens. He had learned to keep his motor running and, when she took breath, to slide away in apologetic surprise at the behavior of his vehicle. But now she soothed him. He braked and listened while Mrs Purdy talked on and on.

She talked of everything under her sun, from Purdy's sweet tooth to her troubles with the heifer. Out of one week of her life in the country she spun a narrative worthy of Marco Polo and, when personal anecdote ran dry, she called up the testimony of relatives, of whom she seemed to possess hundreds living and dead and invariably one among them, however she diversified her subjects, a witness to the gospel truth. What a senator she would make, thought Trimble—what a filibuster!

"Can you come?" said Mrs Purdy. He sat up straight, roused more by her pause than her question.

"I beg your pardon, I'm afraid I was thinking——"

"To the Harvest Home," said Mrs Purdy, "tonight at the church. The Methodists are giving theirs tonight; next week it's the Presbyterians and the week after the Calvary Brethren. We all use the church basement, which some of the old folks don't approve, but seeing Little Salem ain't got but one church and everybody going to everybody else's Harvest Home, well, I call it real friendly and no more than Christianlike, I always say—— How do, Pearly?"

"How do, Mrs Purdy?"

Trimble had not heard the child. He looked up to catch her defiant stare, and though he smiled, trying to atone for snubbing her back there on the road, not a glimmer answered him and no remote acknowledgment, as she trudged on in the dust, that he might be watching her still, unless it was something in her walk, a lift, a whip as unchildlike and challenging as her stare. In the same moment he became aware of two things: that he was, in truth, goggling after her like a sailor ashore and that, for the last half minute, Mrs Purdy had not said a word. But if it was he who flushed, it was Mrs Purdy who jumped when he broke the silence.

"Is that one of the neighbor's——"

"Havla's daughter," said Mrs Purdy. Trimble waited but she did not go on. Out of the corner of his eye he remarked her tight lips and, embarrassed, he started the car. Mrs Purdy put out her hand and held onto the windshield.

"Now don't you run off without my mincemeat—I won't be a shake——"

When he drove up the lane with the jar of mincemeat bouncing beside him his emotions bounced too. He could laugh at her and be touched by her kindness, weary of her chatter yet be embarrassed by its absence. And she had looked so wistful when he took himself away. ... Trimble, you dog, you ought to be shot for not letting her talk you stiff.

The farm comforted him; in the heat of the day it was a sanctuary. He was not glad when John Faith's car followed his up the hill.

6

John Faith got out alone. With cocked head he surveyed the house before he crossed to the shade of the big oak.

"It looks good," he said.

Bone by bone, as if they might suddenly part at the joints, as if they were infinitely precious and fragile, he laid his six feet on the grass.

"I'll get you a pillow," said Trimble. "I'll tell Laurence you're staying for lunch."

"No," said John Faith, "no lunch. I suppose the day may come when I will eat again. I suppose—as this little strength begins to ebb—if they don't tell me first—and if they hold me—I suppose I will submit to forcible feeding.... I don't want a pillow either. But you might give me a drink."

"There was this fellow Slope," said John Faith when he had drunk his drink. "Harvey Slope. You've met him. Runs the paper in Madison. He had these friends of his out from town he knew when he was a reporter. Fellow name Binyon—publicity counselor—he practically put on the World's Fair, to hear him tell it. And Binyon's wife and Mrs Binyon's girl friend, Mrs Catesby, Gladys Catesby..."

He sighed, thumbing the night's beard on his ruddy skin. "I always sort of liked the name Gladys too," he said sadly.

His blue eyes stared into the oak, and Trimble, looking down into their whites, only faintly bloodshot, thought how all of John Faith's stories began the same way, always "this fellow Slope," as though he were someone John Faith had but just met, whereas Trimble knew they were boon companions; last week, last night, the last drink—"this fellow Slope."

"Binyon," said John Faith, "wanted to buy a farm. At least that was the general idea. Just a little place in the country where he could get away from it all. You know—nothing elaborate—nothing fancy—a couple, or maybe a couple of hundred, acres—house with six or eight, or maybe twenty, rooms—garage and servants' quarters—off the highway, but not too far off—bath, electricity, steam heat, telephone—that's all. He didn't want a lake or a hunting preserve or his own landing field; he just wanted a little farm. And he was willing to pay ten thousand dollars for it."

John Faith paused. "Ten thousand dollars," he repeated sadly.

"But first," he said, "Binyon wanted a drink. He wanted a drink before he wanted a farm, and so—thanks, Laurence, I could use another—we all went over to Harve's house.

"This was yesterday afternoon, you understand, along about two o'clock when they got out here. I guess Binyon needed a drink. I guess Binyon needed a drink as bad as I do. I guess he hadn't had a drink since the last stop ten miles back. Mrs Binyon said poor Herbert had been out late the night before working for that awful fair. Poor Herbert just leered at me when she said it. Mrs Binyon said as far as that went, she wouldn't mind having a drink. I don't know what Mrs Binyon had been doing the night before, but she didn't get that breath darning poor Herbert's socks. Gladys—Mrs Catesby—didn't say anything—then.

"Well, like I said, we all went over to Harve's house and had a drink. We had several drinks, and it was along about the second drink that Mrs Catesby introduced us to her friends, the Lingleys. The Lingleys weren't there, you understand—Mrs Catesby said they were at the Atlantic Beach Club at that very moment; the way she looked at me it was somehow my fault that she wasn't at the Atlantic Beach Club too—but something about Harve's house, it was the Dutch doors or the wallpaper or maybe it was just a bottle, reminded her of the Lingleys' place—which I don't need to tell you was on Long Island—and we were killing the fourth drink before she got us off the Lingleys' terrace into the Lingleys' house. She was going right on, right through the forty-six rooms and twenty-nine baths, if I hadn't suggested that Binyon's farm might look better if we saw it by daylight. Bad as he wanted another drink, Herbert said yes and we all got up and got started.

"Binyon wanted to drive his own car—it was a Cadillac, a swell white job with red trimmings, brand new—but I persuaded him to go in mine; told him the roads into some of these places might scratch his paint."

John Faith shook with dry, mirthless laughter.

"Excuse me," he said while Trimble refilled his glass. "I can't help it when I think of Herbert's paint."

He drank.

"I guess," he meditated, "I guess I showed those folks fifteen farms. I guess I showed them pretty nearly all the farms between Madison and the river. After a while I got to showing them farms I knew weren't for sale, places I knew the owners wouldn't mind or they were away. I even showed them J. T. Gasford's farm, with the grilled windows from Italy and the Guernseys he bought for two thousand dollars a head. We didn't go in. I priced it to Binyon at seven thousand cash—I wish old man Gasford could have heard me!—and Herbert didn't even stop yawning. By that time, you see, he was as fed up as I was.

"It was all on account of this dame Gladys," said John Faith and he closed his eyes. "Gladys! Mrs Catesby!...She couldn't stop talking. She was as bad as Mrs Purdy down the hill there. And all she could talk about was her friends, the Lingleys, and their place on Long Island; please God, come invasion, it will go with the first blast.

"If I showed them a farm with a brook, the Lingleys had a swimming pool, a trout stream and a yacht basin. If I showed them a pretty swell oil burner, the Lingleys wouldn't use oil heat for their kennels. If my farms raised corn, the Lingleys raised all their own vegetables and orchids to boot; if my farms bred chickens, the Lingleys bred chickens and turkeys and ducks and ostriches; if my farms were just picturesque old rocky farms, the Lingleys had rocks big as battleships. I ask you!

"Well, the funny part of it was that Mrs Binyon didn't get sore. In fact she started agreeing with Gladys every time Gladys opened her trap—yes, Gladys was right, this simply wouldn't do; yes, Gladys knew what she was talking about; yes, Gladys this and Gladys that. So by the shank of the afternoon practically all the talking was being done by those two women, and me and Binyon were just glumming along, hating them and hating each other and hating the hell out of rural America. I knew by then that selling a farm to Binyon would be harder than selling matzoth to Hitler, but I kept going.

"Another funny thing, I began to sense after a while that everything wasn't as sweet between those two women as it seemed to be. I can't tell you how I knew it, because it wasn't a thing either of them said or the way either of them looked, but it dawned on me all at once that this agreeable stuff Mrs Binyon was spilling was strictly phony, that she really hated Mrs Catesby and Mrs Catesby hated her worse than me and Binyon hated each other, that they were whetting their tomahawks and tuning up their war whoops all the time they were carrying on like two sucking doves and that if either one of them suddenly decided to stop pretending, they would need more room than a farm to fight it out in.

"That was the way it was, and that was the way it stayed till we got back to Madison where we'd promised to meet Harve at Valley Inn. This fellow Slope, he's too smart to go hunting farms with his friends."

John Faith opened one blue eye. "You know Harve, don't you? He's a pretty good guy when he's sober and he generally manages to keep his nose clean when he's crocked. But there are times... When we walked in, our own liquor had died on us too long ago to be funny and I was so glad to see a drink I didn't tumble right away that Harve had a beautiful can on. He must have been working it up all the time we were marching over the scenery, but I didn't know how crocked he was till he began making love to Mrs Binyon.

" 'Sweetheart,' he said, and he leaned across the table and grabbed both her paws, 'did I ever tell you that you ought to be in handcuffs?'

"Watch out, I said to myself, here it comes. It's a regular line with Harve and not a very good line either. It begins with the hands and he works around through various organs to the eyes which always remind him of Evelyn Nesbit's eyes. Harve covered the Thaw case when he was a reporter and he never got over it, and I guess he will die believing Evelyn Nesbit was the most beautiful woman since Hebe. He has that Gibson girl picture of her in his bedroom and he told me once he was going to buy a white bearskin rug but he never did. Sometimes, when he is very crocked, he thinks he owns the rug and he tries to work his line around to the rug, only, as I say, it isn't a very good line. Most of the kids he tries it on never heard of Evelyn Nesbit and by the time Harve gets through explaining her they have walked out on him. Watch out, I said, it's only seven o'clock in the evening but he's going to tell Mrs Binyon about his rug.

"But the funny thing was Mrs Binyon seemed to like his line. Maybe she had heard of Evelyn Nesbit—God knows she was old enough to 've—because she said to Harve, 'I think you're cute; isn't he cute?' she said to Gladys, and that was all Harve needed. He got up and moved across the booth next to Mrs Binyon and I told the waitress to bring another round for the four of us. Binyon had wandered away after the first drink. Maybe the drinks weren't coming fast enough for him in the booth, or maybe he was fed up with the rest of us, or maybe he really wanted to see a man about a dog like he said. Anyway, what the hell, I thought, if he wants to lap up his at the bar, that's his business. What the hell, if it's a lost day and I can't sell him a farm, maybe I can get something else out of it. What the hell, I said, let Harve make Mrs Binyon, I'll make Gladys!"

John Faith sat up. He rubbed one ear.

"I don't know if this will sound entirely clear to you," he said. "I mean, what happened. It isn't entirely clear to me. We had all these drinks and Harve was urging Mrs Binyon to go over and see his rug, and I think I was working on Gladys, when Binyon came back. He came back with the waitress and some more drinks and he was standing there leering at us and hugging the waitress when Gladys said 'Herbert!' right past my chin. Binyon went on hugging the waitress and Mrs Binyon got up and said to Gladys, 'Are you making a play for my husband?' and Gladys said, 'You mean your husband that is making a play for that waitress?' and Mrs Binyon said, 'I mean you, you bitch,' and threw her drink at Gladys, and Binyon laughed and tried to kiss the waitress, and Gunderson, the bartender, who is one of the biggest guys in the

Valley and the waitress's husband, came in and knocked Binyon right over the skeeball game.

"I never did know," said John Faith, "exactly what happened after that because I left. I believe Harve was trying to explain to Gunderson that Binyon was a friend of his and didn't mean it. Mrs. Binyon was crying and carrying on over Binyon and the waitress was dabbing poor Herbert with a towel. I remember Gladys asked me to take her back to New York. I was real polite about it, too, considering she had cost me the commission on ten thousand dollars. 'I'm awfully sorry, Mrs Catesby,' I said, 'I'm awfully sorry but I've got a date to show some people some farms,' and I went out and fell in my car and hit a back road and the first field I came to I drove in and crawled on the back seat and went to sleep."

Trimble studied his shut eyes.

"Do you always sleep in fields?" he said. "It seems to me whenever I hear the end of your social evenings——"

"Oh no," said John Faith, "there are nights and nights, between the times I see you, I sleep at home in a bed.

"It is only," he went on without opening his eyes, "when I get mixed up with this fellow Slope that I get into a jam. I went by to see Harve this morning, but he wasn't there. Harve's nigger said he had gone to Somerville. He said Harve got a telephone call. He said he guessed the telephone call had something to do with some of Mr Slope's friends who came by the house last night and drank up all Mr Slope's liquor. He said the friends left about midnight when the gentleman insisted on driving to New York. He said the telephone call came about six o'clock and Mr Slope was mighty mad and cussed his friends all the time he was dressing. So I dropped into Madison and one of the troopers told me this red-and-white Cadillac left the road two miles this side of Somerville and wrecked a milk truck, a telephone pole and a road stand and, though none of the people were bad hurt, he said, they were all in the hospital or the jail charged with everything from drunken driving to resisting arrest, and he guessed Harve Slope would have a tough time squaring this ticket. I guess he will too."

<h1 style="text-align:center">7</h1>

Trimble waited but John Faith said no more. Sprawled where the sunshine warmed his crossed, rumpled ankles, he did not look like a tavern brawler or a go-getter who doggedly pursued his living through three counties; he looked like the little boy Trimble had surprised in those moments when John Faith talked of his beagles or his zinnias.

"Are you asleep?" he said, and when John Faith's head moved gingerly on the grass, "What I don't understand is, why do they do it? These people from New York, they probably really wanted a farm; they wanted something their life as it is couldn't give them, and here it was, a dream come true perhaps, but they had to befoul it and murder it and cheat themselves out of it by making it exactly like the life they were running away from. And you and Harvey Slope, you're just as bad. Why do you do it?"

John Faith said, yawning, "Because we're frustrated," and Trimble laughed.

"Don't you ever get tired of that word? I notice you trot it out whenever you want to duck the issue. All right—you're frustrated—Slope's frustrated—I'm frustrated——"

"Sure," yawned John Faith, "everybody's frustrated."

Trimble gazed across the Valley.

"I don't believe it," he said. "John, who are the people that run the store in Little Salem?"

"The Gillibos? Frustrated."

"They're not very sociable anyway. I couldn't get three words out of him, and when she came in——"

"Ah," said John Faith. Trimble, looking down, saw that the lips below the closed eyes smiled. "Emil's jealous."

Trimble snorted. He wanted to tell John Faith that the color of all creation is not pink because rye whisky runs red; he wanted to say that the world is rainbowed to infinity yet its spectrum can be caught in tiny prisms. He watched the Valley shimmer.

"Want another drink, John?"

"No," said John Faith, "but if you don't mind, I'll use your grass and your oak tree for a while, and maybe a razor after that. Wake me up come cocktail time. I gotta show some folks some farms."

CHAPTER TWO
LITTLE SALEM: NOON

AFTER the door slammed neither the man nor the woman spoke until the crunches in the gravel ceased and the motor started and its beat dwindled beyond earshot. The woman spoke then into the dim, hot silence.

She said, without emphasis but implacably, "How much did he give you?"

The man said, "You were here."

He had not relaxed his fixed position, drawn and upright against the shelves, and now he did not relax or cringe or alter it in any way as she crossed the room, walking straight, firmly, with a sure tap of her high heels, like a woman entering her favorite department store. When she stopped she stopped easily on both heels, on both hips, as only women do who are confident of symmetry.

"How much?"

The man, not answering, not moving, yet seemed to draw tighter. The skin across his frontal bone was the color of catgut twisted on a peg. He looked as if he waited to be struck.

"How much?" said the woman, a foot from him across the counter.

The man said, not looking at her, "That's my business."

The woman struck him. Her flat palm, returning clenched to her side, left its print white against his cheek. Blood slowly suffused the mottles. The blood went up, dyeing the closed eyelids and the yellow forehead.

"You peewee," said the woman, the violence in her voice as soft as fur. "Sure, I was here. Sure, I heard him come in, right after the kid. Do you think I watch you every minute? Do you think I listened? I don't care what you do with the kid—you peewee! Do you think I spied on you and him?"

The man began to say, whining it, "Now, Selena——"

"Oh, shut up," said the woman; she said it almost good-naturedly. "How much did he give you?"

The man withdrew one hand from his pants pocket and laid a dollar on the counter. Her scrutiny of the bill became whimsical.

"Good god," she yawned.

"I had to give him thirty cents change," said the man.

"Good god," repeated the woman in the same amused drawl. "That rich drip finally comes in here and you soak him for a dozen bananas, a sack of flour and a dime's worth of peas. Oh, sure I heard it—I just wanted to see if you'd lie for seventy cents. Seventy cents! And he'll go down to Madison and squander enough to buy you out."

"Now, Selena," said the man, spreading his hand, "he didn't ask——"

The woman whirled on him. Her furious voice did not ascend a minor interval.

"You could have sold him half the stuff in the place; you could have got him for the summer; you could have made more out of him in one day than your dirty farmers spend in a year. You've watched him boggling by in that moving-picture Packard—going down to Madison—going up to his place—spending money like a fool—getting swindled by every nitwit who can split a shingle—till you were lathered up like Purdy's bull thinking what you were missing. You peewee! And then the first chance you get at him, you run him out of here so fast he wouldn't come back for bug poison if bugs were eating him alive. What's the matter with you? Haven't you got what it takes?—even to snuggle up to money?"

A glistening quality appeared in the man's face. It was visible in the gloom. He opened his eyes and shut them again.

"You were here," he said.

"Oh, shut up." The woman made a casual hand's pass at her smooth black hair. "I'm not going to hit you. If I was here, it wasn't for lack of you trying to get him out first." She resumed her drawl; there was a kind of mocking satisfaction in it. "Why didn't I snuggle up to him? Maybe I should have. But he wasn't my customer, he was yours." She addressed a side of bacon hanging among the festoons of flypaper. "He likes to wait on people— he even likes to wait on little girls."

The man glistened. He said nothing.

She said chattily, "Say, Emil, you think he's a nance? Not the way he talks, but there's always something about them when they look at a woman——"

She was circling the room in slow, easy paces.

"Maybe not. Maybe he's a he-man. With that car...and all that money...He looks strong too."

Suddenly she pinned the man's hand where it crept toward the bill. Her stare lasted till his own eyes fogged into their cataleptic blank. When she had put the bill in the pocket of her dress she tossed her head as a cow might which has fed to stuffiness. At the curtain she spoke.

"You peewee," she said softly as she went out.

The man, after a moment, rubbed his hands.

2

Her heel taps made no sound on the carpet as Selena entered the room where Grandfather Gillibo sat. But he looked up instantly and his blind face ferreted her out; his quaver reached her before she had taken three steps: "Can I play it now, S'lena?" She turned aside to put in the plug and instantly the old man's fingers clawed the dials. Bombilation roared into the silence.

The fingers twittered; a voice cut the din: "And when I say this glorious count-tree——" The old man lurched his head into the machine's mouth while an expression of lickerish joy daubed his gums. The voice roared on.

In the kitchen Selena tied on an apron, opened the refrigerator and took out a dish of cold cabbage and a paper of chops. The chops were pork, meager, sleazy and two thirds fat. She dumped these into a skillet which she first greased and placed over a flame on the gas stove. From a shelf she picked one of a dozen cans, opening it on the drainboard where she had left the cabbage. The beans slid gluily into a saucepan. She pitched the can into a crate under the sink, put the saucepan over a second flame and turned the four chops which were sizzling.

In the next room the roaring voice expired in a gust of handclapping, and band music submerged both. Selena began to set the table.

She set two places, cups, plates, knives, forks and spoons, a bowl of sugar, butter from the refrigerator. Immediately flies buzzed above the bowl. She waved them away and began to slice bread. When she had stacked it and brought the plate to the table two flies were in the butter and the bowl swarmed. She forked out the struggling flies, flicked at the others and covered both dishes. The flies returned to stalk the bare china unmolested. Selena jabbed two holes with the icepick in a can of condensed milk and added it to the flies' objectives.

The band music changed to a confusion of instrumental and vocal noises, topped by a repeated metallic clang. This went on for some time.

A large coffeepot, black to the snout, already stood on the stove. Selena took it off, swished it, peered inside and at the tap dashed water into the pot before she returned it to the stove. Her lips, which had been as impassive as her black arched brows, for the first time moved. Their curl might have been vexation or scorn. Her tongue slipped out and back, licking perspiration.

A little restively she poked the chops, transferred two to a platter and slewed the cold cabbage in with the other chops and the bubbling grease. Then she wiped her wet face on the apron, walked to the door and across the uproar of music, voices and static cried "Emil!"

She called him again after she had pulled out the plug and helped Mr Gillibo to his feet. By the time she had guided the old man across the carpet, hobbling her stride to his shuffle and gripping his elbows like rudders because she was less impatient doing it that way than having him butting and banging with his stick, her husband had appeared behind them, trailing them wordlessly to the kitchen and waiting, standing flatly to his chair, while his grandfather wobbled and clattered into his and she, wordless, too, untied her apron and fixed it about the old man's neck and shook the folds over his lap.

"Ain't you having any dinner?" said Emil Gillibo.

"You know I'm not," she said. She went on serving the food.

When they were both eating she heated water in a fresh saucepan and made tea and shook small hard crackers out of a box, but she had to stop twice to tend the old man because a forkful spilled and once when he lifted his petulant, trembling chin.

"No preserves, S'lena?"

She got down the jar of preserves and opened it and spooned them out, shooing away the flies, and while her tea steeped went into the store and came back with an oiled packet of cake which she sliced into halves, putting a hunk on each plate. She bent over the old man.

"It's cake!" she shouted. "Cake!"

Grandfather Gillibo, at the preserves, made noises of grateful understanding. She patted his back.

When she had poured her tea and paused at the door with the cup in one hand and the crackers in the other she spoke to her husband in her natural voice.

"You're not shy about eating it a bit, are you?"

Emil Gillibo rarely looked startled. He did now. Above the leavings of his beans and cabbage he gaped at her.

"Shy?"

"Yes. It might be"—she smiled brightly before she left him with the thought—"full of arsenic."

3

She married Emil Gillibo in 1926, when she was twenty.

He was French or so he said; his race and heritage had never interested her much. The Valley was full of European stock: Swedes, Dutch, Germans, Italians, Poles, Greeks, some of it planted by Hessians after the Revolution, most of it spilled out from the seaboard cities in a century's waves of immigration. There were too many funny names for one more to be remarkable. Besides, everybody's children in the Valley were Americans, except when somebody got mad; then they were the children of those damn wops or polaks. Emil's grandfather, who was born in Brussels and once spelled his name Gillibeaux, was no better or worse than Grandfather Norton, who was born in Brooklyn.

The wedding was in Madison where Emil's father owned the hotel. Emil was the clerk, a frail, silent, sallow youth who did not know how to play baseball and whose dark eyes seemed to carry a mystery and a promise. All the girls said he was so different from the other boys in the Valley.

They went to New York on their honeymoon and Selena saw her first speakeasy and her first ocean liner and in Macy's Misses' Wear spent most of Papa Gillibo's check. After their return to Madison she would urge Emil, every time he grumbled about the hotel, to quit clerking and look for something in New York. They had no children.

But when the depression began and Emil's mother died and Emil's father shot himself they perforce went to the Nortons' in Little Salem. After the hotel's creditors got through with Emil

Selena's uncle sold Emil the store. It was the first cash money Uncle Cliff had handled in months and the last Emil had in the world. Selena, moving in their furniture and the trunk with the clothes she had bought in New York four years before, could see from an upper window the house where she was born.

Standing by one of the twin beds she had bullied Emil into buying, she looked at the peeling gables for several minutes, motionless except for a sudden contraction of her muscular legs. The twilight deepened. She tossed her hat on a chair and tramped downstairs. Grandfather Gillibo stood up in the creamery truck, holding by one hand to his radio. "S'lena!" he cried out. She helped him down and inside.

Later, when the old man had fed and sat in the dark with WJZ turned on full power, she entered the store. Emil was arranging stock. He turned, frowning, and she sensed, through long intuition to his taciturnities, why he frowned.

"Let him be," she said. "If he don't use your electricity to see by, you needn't begrudge him the juice to hear. I'll put up with him," she said; "I'll put up with that," gesturing as the noise fulminated around her. She came close enough to forego shouting. "But there's something I want you to know, Emil; it's been working on me for a long time and you better know it now. I'm not putting up with anything else." When he only blinked at her she repeated "Anything!" in that softly violent voice he had learned not to answer. She then used for the first time the word she was not to forget thereafter. "You peewee!" she sneered and saw his breath suck in.

The folk of Little Salem, including her Norton kin, soon discovered that Selena Gillibo was not one of them. She had been bred in their Valley, schooled in its ways, bound by its outlook and tempered in its inescapable seasons. But Mrs Gillibo did not attend church; she did not return their calls; their hospitality went evaded or unreciprocated; outside of the store they never saw Mrs Gillibo except going away or coming back in Emil's Ford.

At first they were resentful. Had she committed a hostile act or an open sin, the women would have stopped speaking to her. But the worst they had "on" her was her reply to the Rev Mr Featherstone when he chided her for backsliding. "Church makes me kind of sick," Selena was reported to have said, a defense which had nonplused Mr Featherstone's theology.

Gradually the women stopped calling on Mrs Gillibo; gradually they stopped asking her to their missionary meetings and their sociables. But they continued to speak, to go to the store, where Mrs Gillibo would greet them impassively and impassively wait on them and listen impassively to their homely, rollicking chatter until something in her face discomfited and daunted them. They would feel that Mrs Gillibo must regard them as if they were all like Mr Havla, who paid his taxes but was a "foreigner," someone whose language you didn't understand and who couldn't be expected to understand yours. But that was all right, too, for as a foreigner was exactly the way in which they finally came to regard Selena Gillibo.

The members of the Ladies' Aid Society, straggling by ones and twos along Main Street, bowed to Selena on her front porch and some of them waved.

Selena bowed back. She did not wave. She sipped her tea and bit her hard little crackers and without expression watched the ladies approach through the strong sun, their scramble up the path by the slumbering cemetery and their invariable pause, like actresses in the wings, before they disappeared into the shadow with their sacrifices of chicken, salads and jellies.

Once or twice she confused a white dress with a headstone. She smiled at the thought before the fury in her mind shut it out.

4

So had they slumbered in their pink casket ... the little bottles ... six of them ... ebony black with little scarlet crowns ... labeled

Cyclamen, Narcissus, Heather, Amaryllis, Anemone and Mignonette...like the names of six little princesses waiting to be waked...and on either side the jars...crystalline, glittering, a double row...of lotions, unguents, astringents, powders...to pat and rub and smooth and dust...until they worked their sorcery...and the little boxes...eye shadow, mascara, rouge...and the implements...little brushes, little tweezers...silvery...all, like the little bottles, cuddled in pink, slumbering on satin, waiting for the waking touch.

When she had first seen them in McKasker's window in Madison they had halted her like magic out of a fairy tale. And now, as they rippled toward her through the July weather, flashing their iridescence in the waves of her fancy, it seemed unbelievable that this whole enchantment could be confined in a leather case no bigger than a ham. Selena put down her teacup and began to rock. No bigger than a ham...

...and no costlier than the dirty hog it takes to make a ham. Dear God, must I go the rest of my days tied to the cash in a country store and the credit sunk in a neighbor's pigpen? It isn't as though they were such a much, like a new car for that junk pile he couldn't swap for peanuts, or real jewelry, or the swell dresses in the magazines, or that fur coat she'd had on in the movie. Deanna Durbin. Just a kid. Sixteen, they say. Why, when you were sixteen you were wearing your mother's old cloth coat and crazy about it because you knew you looked swell the way the boys stared and because, when you were sixteen, you knew that someday you would have fur coats and, oh, everything, and not be beating your brains out to grub up twenty dollars...

The chair beat back and forth.

...twenty dollars for something a lot of women could get with a nod to a salesgirl. Make-up kits they call them in the beauty advice and maybe those swell places, Elizabeth Arden, Dorothy Gray, Helena Rubenstein, with all that talk about "youthful, exquisite transluscence" and too snotty to tell you the price, maybe they treat those society bitches with something special, but I bet I can get just as good out of the jars … and the little bottles … Cyclamen … Amaryllis … dear God!

… of course you can buy them cheaper, as low as three dollars, but no perfumes, no gadgets, no little brushes and tweezers … and awfully cheap creams, I bet; why, hell, I wouldn't put that cheap stuff on my skin; I'd use soap and water first; skin's too important; it's too lovely … lovely, he had said, you have lovely skin, and for a second you thought he was going to kiss you, right there at the bar and Emil on your other side squirming like he was in diapers, so you said to Emil he's just a drunk and you went on back to the hotel but thinking all the time it is nice, nice to be told instead of waiting like a lump till somebody gets good and ready and nothing much said then or much done either and remembering still how you got up after Emil went to sleep and slipped to the bathroom and studied yourself in the mirror and, later, in the dark, stroked yourself gently, gently … oh, the hell with that!

She rocked furiously.

Much good it does to think what a fool you were thirteen years ago; what matters now is getting the money, get every cent he tries to hide but, my God, what have you got when you get it and whoever would have thought thirteen years ago things would turn out the way they did and I don't mean just the old man or the store or Little Salem or even Emil, the poor slob, but the whole mess, the whole godawful mess, days and nights and years of it, cold, mud, stink, sweat, nobody to talk to, nobody talking to you except that damn radio, and the eternal kitchen, and every room hot as blazes or cold as ice and you trying to stay clean, trying to keep young, trying to be yourself … for what?

The rocker stopped.

… I dunno. It's just nature, I guess, it's mine anyhow, to fight anything and anybody that tries to dirty you, the husband in your bed or the other men that want to be there—the cheap bastards. ... No, thanks, Mr Faith, no, thanks, Mr Slope, and all the rest of you with your city ideas and your country two bits; why, before I'd take a chance with you and get my name dirtied the length of the Valley I'd give it away; I'd pick me a clean kid just for the fun of it. ... I'd stop a stranger ... one of those truck drivers ... or some city man passing through; they say it happens all the time at the tourist camps ... at the taverns ... those waitresses ... with men passing through ... for a lot more than twenty dollars ...

Selena sat still in her chair.

The high sun stood as still in its molten sky, blistering the earth till the tar bubbled where the macadam ran out of Little Salem. Shadows gripped the boles of trees and under the porch roof danced in lines as visible as the waves on a graph. By and by they would lengthen, reaching out from the dogwoods and syringas across the scrubby yards; Uncle Cliff Norton would emerge with his hose; the kids would start playing in the lot where the canning factory used to be, and down at their pasture bars Romerly's cows would set up a plaintive lowing. When fireflies winked a light would go on in one room of the Norton house and, as if this were a signal, in a window of each house along the tiny street. As the first farmer rattled in to barter his eggs for staples night would fall, hot in the small rooms where bugs and moths battered at the screens, cool presently outside, but in or out as black, as enfolding as the dark that shut in the sleepers over yonder.

Into the eyes that weighed them and the street and the houses and all that knit her inextricably to them water slowly welled, quenching the fury, drowning the hatred and the hard calculation. A tear splashed down Selena Gillibo's nose. "Home, sweet home," she said aloud, "you poor sap," and knocked the tears away with one rough motion.

She got up, rubbing her cheeks, as the radio in the house behind her resumed its roar. She did not hear the second noise until it was too late to cry out. Yet cry out she did, planting her high heels on the stoop, lifting a fist into the sun.

"Come back here, Emil! Come back with that Ford!"

The Ford careened on until dust and sun hid it.

CHAPTER THREE
THE BARRENS:
AFTERNOON

WHEN Joe was nearing the end of the last furrow a cock pheasant walked out of the woods into the young corn, stepping high and handsome and as unafraid as if he had been a million miles away. Glory blue and gold and red, it paused not ten yards beyond the horses to peck at a knee-high stalk. It shook its beak exactly as people do when something sticks in their teeth; a wisp of green floated away and the cock stepped along as much as to say, "Damn stuff's not ripe yet." He had heard that the pheasants ate the corn but he had never seen such a sight with his own eyes. He laughed aloud and at once the cock took wing, soaring gracefully till its trailing tail was a wisp like the husk against the dazzling hot horizon. Later, going down the road, the horses almost ran down a hen bird, her brood scuttering and cheeping around her.

If he had had his gun, what a sweet shot the cock would have been. But by November, when the season opened, try and find him! He would be gone from there, and every other pheasant with him. Those buggers were so smart that the first hunter, waking the Barrens, ran them to cover as surely as though he had sent them a telegram. A fellow was lucky if he got a cock a season nowadays.

Unhitching the horses from the cultivator, he thought about the cock in the corn and about the cock he would shoot in the fall. It would be wonderful then, with harvests in and the fields cleared and nothing to bother about but odd jobs and the stock. He could be gone a whole day sometimes, working west against the wind if it was right, up over the Barrens into the wild part where no land had been plowed for years and the sumac and the brambles made miles of game coverts almost as far as the Delaware. Funny, when you got going, how a fellow didn't much care whether he shot a pheasant or not. It was always there, just ahead, enough in itself to lead you on, the chance of a sudden whir and the quick, pressed trigger.

Once he had shot a pheasant in late November, just before Thanksgiving. There had been a light snowfall, not enough to lawlessly track game but drifted here and there in hollows and coverts. He had been out all day with no luck but a couple of rabbits and this bird came out of snow like a white ghost bursting the twilight. The dogs must have run right over it where it bedded under a drift and he himself trod so close that snow showered him. For an instant the particles stung and he fired blindly, scarcely knowing what he shot at. But the bird fell and when he got there, shouting at the pouncing dogs, it was a fine cock. He would never forget it: the burst and the gunfire almost together; the hit; triumph; Thanksgiving dinner for sure; the beauty of the reddening plumage on the white freckled ground, all twisted into one shivering thrill in the lowering day's end.

Now some people would say a fellow was downright mean to feel that way. You take his mother—for all they depended on game like city people do on the butcher, she wouldn't look at that bird when he brought it in. Made him dress it in the yard and wouldn't hear to having the tail on the plate, though she saved it afterward because, she said, it was pretty. She was just as tender about that bird as she was about her own chickens. He or Pop had to wring a chicken's neck every time, and do all the rest of it right down to the oven, and she would never let them tell her which one it was till she found it out for herself next day, mourning to herself and never mentioning the missing chicken's name again. She had names for all of them, Old Biddy and Bettywee and names like that. But when the chicken was on the table he noticed she ate it, Bettywee or not.

Well, you take people like that, they say killing's justified because you've got to eat. But that isn't the whole answer; it doesn't explain the feeling you get when wings burr and you let go both barrels and, just when you think you've missed, a bird drops. Maybe there is something cruel in it. Maybe it's the same cruelty a gangster feels when he gives a guy the works or a G-man when he shoots a gangster. He couldn't shoot a guy in cold blood, but he could let him have it if the guy was a gangster and he him-self was Dick Tracy. Maybe that was it. Pheasants are outlaws; they're fleeing and the law says let 'em have it. So you bang away to get your bird and it doesn't much matter who eats it, any more than it does to Dick Tracy whether a guy burns or beats the rap. You got it—that was the thrill.

He slapped the horses' wet rumps and whistled to the dogs, panting on their sides under the big cherry, and the two hounds got up and shook themselves and waited until he and the horses came abreast before they trailed out of the shade into the field, moving gingerly among the clods as if their pads, their drooped ears, their listless tails rebelled at the hot earth and the need to follow him. His own ears dripped at the lobes; his shirt, though bleached by many washings, was dark with sweat; sweat squashed in his boots. But he hadn't minded the sun while he worked or while he thought about the cock red in the cool snow and he didn't really mind it now, thinking only, gee, it's some Fourth of July; it's a blister all right.

It was so hot that the baked ground almost refused the steel and, unless rain came soon, the corn would shrivel on the stalks. But rain would come, it always did on the Barrens, and out of just such a burning sky as this. He had seen it come in midsummer so swiftly that you could light a match from a rock as from a stove and the next minute have the flame extinguished by a hissing torrent. And on other days, when fog choked the Barrens till you couldn't see the barn from the back door, you were as likely as not to get a sunstroke when you led out the first cow.

Yes sir, like the fellow said in that book his father used to read, the weather hereabouts was always doing something, but the weather suited him with all its spasms, the snow and the sun, the fog, the rains, the black frosts of January, the muds of March, even the thunderstorms rumbling out of Copperhead Gap to break with a crackle and a crash that sent most folks dashing to the cellar. Why, when he was just a kid he wanted to run out into the rain to catch the lightning. He had never been afraid of it, not even after Holland Heinschmidt got killed.

He and Holland were buddies. Together they had worked the fields and reaped the crops, hunting together, roaming together, snuffing out each other's hearts as intimately as those two dogs there. But Holland had not been like him inside. He remembered, when they went to Washington with the senior class, how the city had excited them and awed them and kindled in them a proper patriotism. But he remembered best coming home.

"And what was Washington like, boys?" his mother had demanded when they tramped up the long road from the bus.

"Hard on the feet," he had answered, and let Holland talk. For he could not explain to his mother why the dirt of the Valley felt sweeter to his bruised heels than all the hallowed ground in Arlington.

Holland had not loved the land. He said he hated it; he said when he got through high school he was going away the day he graduated. He said he was going to Texas and learn to fly and become a transport pilot and see places like Hollywood and Panama and the Far East. When they read about Redfearn being lost in the jungle Holland said he wished it was him. If it was, he said, he would start a secret empire among the Amazonian Indians and teach them to build planes and fly, and then he would conquer North and South America and rule them with a beautiful queen like the girl in Flash Gordon. Holland swore he would bomb all farms and the Heinschmidt farm the first of all.

He had been shocked listening to Holland, and when the Amazonian dictator lay with his battered milk pail at the foot of the tall pear tree his first thought was that God had heard and acted. Staring down at the livid face and the stuff like sawdust welling out of Holland's chest, and even a month afterward, when the stricken tree bloomed again and he wondered if Holland, too, bloomed under the grass of Little Salem cemetery, he was conscious through his mourning for Holland of a horrible gladness that the Heinschmidt farm was not to be bombed.

For the farm had been his farm, more his than Holland's. He knew every stump and gully on it; not a twist of the lane but stirred in him some daydream out of the past. The dreams stayed vivid and Holland became the faint shadow. So, when the Heinschmidts moved away, he had a dream that his father might buy the farm. But strangers from Philadelphia bought it and all one summer he watched their swift, forbidding cars whip past; once, idling across the fields, he was ordered off by a hard, dark man in a derby hat. Months later, after the strangers, too, had moved away, he found their still in the woods, its coils as rusty as the machines in the decaying barn. He wrecked it and trucked the pieces off the land and after that the Heinschmidt farm lay fallow.

The rains ruled it and the snows and the gnawing frosts. The sun ruled with the rains. Rivulets gashed the fields and spilled into the lane, cutting the crossovers and digging ruts into little chasms. They carried the topsoil with them, leaving the rocks, and where soil stayed between the rocks and the rivulets and the sun cracks the weeds took hold and bush grass and vines and at last the sumac, marching in steady clumps and files. By the time Trimble acquired the farm, green jungle hid the ravage. But no bombs had done a rougher job.

And who was this Trimble? A fellow, obviously, who cared more about getting his hair cut than his hay, who had to call for a plumber if a pipe leaked, who talked about books at breakfast and began a fine morning in a monkey chair, smacking at bumblebees. Oh, Trimble was all right—Trimble had rebuilt the house; he had cleared the lawn; he had given them the fields for nothing, speaking vaguely of sharing their vegetables as if they had not patiently explained that the corn would be good only for fodder—Trimble was all right as far as he went. But you could see easy enough he was no help to the land; he was about as helpful as the bull in the funny picture who liked to sit on his ass and smell flowers.

Hell, if he owned the Heinschmidt farm, what wouldn't he do with it! Fields fenced, roads graveled, buildings spanking new, model dairy, barns as big as factories, chicken coops like apartment houses; machines! He'd have tractors and harrows and reapers better than those in the newsreels of the great farms out West. His fruit trees would be nursed and sprayed like show dogs. His stock would be fatter and finer than a fair's. His crops would make your eyes bug out. He'd have a hundred men working for him and show 'em all what working was. Hell, he'd have him a farm!

Of course, in a manner of speaking, you might say he already had a farm, for someday he would inherit their place as his father had inherited before him when his grandfather died. But owning a farm that way—inheriting, knowing you would inherit, working always with your old man who must die before you could lay claim to the piece of dirt you plowed or the plow handle under your palm—that was worse than owning no farm at all. If it wasn't your farm, you at least got wages, but if it was your old man's farm, you got no wages and you got no satisfaction either, for what satisfaction is there in working for something collectible only at the price of your old man's life?

Working the Heinschmidt farm was different. It wasn't work for wages and it wasn't work for your old man and certainly it wasn't work for a fellow who sat on his pratt and smacked bumblebees while the tent caterpillars ate his orchard. And though you dreamed while you worked that it was your land—same old dream of the little fellow who stared across a dusty road at its greener slopes—still it wasn't work for yourself. He guessed, when you came to think about it, the work was for the land if it was for anybody, bringing it back, healing it, making it bloom and produce and live. Once, before strangers let it rot and desecrated it like sinners in the Bible desecrated holy things, he had seen this land live. And maybe if he worked and dreamed hard enough he would see it live again; fruitful, beautiful, clean—his land.

He turned a bend of the lane, whistling, and John Faith, sitting up, regarded him with the fatalistic stare of a gargoyle who wishes the birds would perch somewhere else.

2

"Do you enjoy it?" said John Faith. "Does it pleasure you in the same way the bark does the dog and bellowing the bull?"

Joe pulled up the horses and smiled on him, all the crinkles he would have at sixty rushing into prophetic, youthful pattern. He said nothing, knowing Mr Faith.

"Because if you do," said John Faith, "I can only say that I am a frustrated man, tone deaf but unfortunately not stone deaf."

He picked a blade of grass and nibbled it and stared blue and faintly bloodshot at the softening east.

"Was a fellow over by Frenchtown," he said. "Whistled all the time. Whistled when he got up in the morning and when he went to bed at night. Whistled at his mealtimes. Whistled when he felt good, whistled when he felt bad, whistled in church, whistled, I suppose, if he jumped in the hay. Never was such a fellow for whistling. Met a fellow in the road one morning and stopped to say something. Opened his mouth to say it and couldn't. Whistled instead. Been whistling ever since. They got him on Broadway in Ripley's Odd-It-Torium."

Joe beamed on the slowly rising bald head.

"What was that fellow's name, Mr Faith?"

"I forget."

John Faith reached his height; he walked to the pickets.

"How are you, Joe?"

They shook hands.

Eastward their shadows merged under the sweating horses' bellies, and the horses' shadows fell with the oaks' into the bordering weeds. The sun dropped a visible scintilla. But the dogs lay in the weeds and panted.

John Faith leaned on the pickets.

"How's tricks, Joe?"

"Okay."

"How's your father?"

"He worries, Mr Faith."

"You tell him," said John Faith, still leaning on the pickets, "to cut it out. I mean the worrying. You tell him I said so. You tell him, if Buckmeister bothers him about that loan, to see me. He's paid his taxes, ain't he?"

"Yes sir—all but last year's."

"That's fair enough. Your father's too good a man to let a little squirt like Buckmeister worry him."

"Yes sir. Thanks, Mr Faith."

The hounds watched them, ears alert, tongues slobbering.

John Faith bit the grass stem and spat it in the road.

"They started dumping milk again over in Essex," he said, and his eyes narrowed. "Jack Pete tells me he can't collect enough for his oil to refill his truck. There's forty farm sales advertised in the *Democrat*. I could buy 'em in at twenty dollars an acre if I had the dough."

"This here's a mighty pretty farm, Mr Faith."

John Faith looked up and he waited.

"I mean it could be a mighty pretty farm," said Joe. "I mean if a fella had the money——"

He stopped. John Faith's blue stare took in the reddening face.

"Jesus Christ," he whispered, "Jesus Christ, he likes it!" His stare increased to a gleam that was the nearest an unrelieved stare could come to irony. He said, "Don't you want to go to New York, Joe? Or Newark? Or Jersey City?"

Joe spoke carefully.

"I'm not horsing to."

"Don't you want good union wages at a dollar and a half an hour—whenever the union will let you work? Don't you want a job on the railroad? Wouldn't you like to wipe windshields at a nice service station? Can't I fix you up in a swell factory with an eight-hour day and a five-day week?"

Joe shook his head.

"No sir."

"Or maybe you'd try out the C C C camp—roof, board and hospitalization—and let the government pay you for leaning on a pick? You could pull down enough to buy you a jallopy and hell around nights and come home week ends and tell the old man how to run the cultivator."

Joe said nothing.

"Don't that appeal to you, Joe? That's what Titcomb's five boys do and they all went to college."

"I know."

"But, good God, Joe, in New York they got a movie on every corner; fellow gets off at five o'clock and nothing to do till tomorrow but get drunk. And they tell me there's so much free tail the women line up 'stead of the men."

Joe grinned.

"I ain't interested," he told the gleam, and again John Faith whispered.

"Jesus Christ," he whispered, "Jesus Christ, he ain't interested."

From the house Trimble's white form appeared under the low porch roof. He busied himself with a cigar and a match while John Faith's voice came indistinctly whimsical across the lawn.

"If I was a fellow loved farming that bad," John Faith was saying, "I'd be scared. I'd be so scared of myself I'd run as far as I could. I'd run me right into town to the first woman I met and I'd say, 'Sweetheart, the cows and the chickens are about to get me; let's me and you have us a time,' and I wouldn't come back till I was dead certain I could feel the sun in my sap at the end of the day without thinking it's a fine night for the Christian Endeavor."

Trimble puffed the cigar, watching those two at the gate. He tossed the burnt match away and stooped and picked it out of the lawn and brushed a little at the spot where it had fallen.

Joe Purdy's eyes braved the gleam.

"It's still a mighty pretty farm," he said. "Do you think, Mr Faith, he"—and he jerked his chin—"he'll ever want to sell?"

John Faith glanced over his shoulder and his right hand went up in salutation.

"Him?" He shook his head. "Not Ferdinand." Then, as Trimble came toward them, he stared again but without irony at Joe Purdy. He said softly, "Don't let 'em get you down, Joe—you keep what you got—all of it."

"Well!" Trimble said. "Well! ... And what are you two talking about?"

3

Going down the lane, he thought about what Mr Faith had said and what a fellow Mr Faith was, always kidding, yet along with the kidding something that made you think maybe he meant it. Didn't know when to believe him and when not to, how much to swallow and how much to take with a grain of salt. Like calling that fellow Ferdinand, which was the name of the bull in the picture. "Not Ferdinand!" they kept saying in the picture and maybe that was all Mr Faith meant, talking like they talked in the picture, but it would be funny if that fellow reminded Mr Faith, too, of a lazy-ass bull. Anyway, that fellow wasn't going to sell the farm, and supposing he did, what was the use of a fellow dreaming of buying a farm when his old man couldn't keep up with the mortgage on his own place? The woods grew thick here and suddenly they seemed to press close; the shade was not cool but only silent and queerly hostile, and Joe came out of the lane, stumbling on the horses' hocks and scowling in the sudden light.

Pearly Havla sat on the corner of the fence, her heels caught in the lower rail. Teetering, she regarded him without surprise.

"Hello," she said.

"Hello, Pearly."

Over the familiar hummock the horses swung into the road to the Purdy barn and he swung with them.

"I seen something nice," she called.

He had to go back on his heels to check the horses.

"What?" he said. "Wha'd you say?"

She did not answer at once. Her small, rigid body balanced an instant like a wire walker's and her gaze fixed itself beyond him.

"I seen something nice. I never seen nothing like it before. It was over there—in the woods."

She pointed, but when he still scowled her finger wavered. She clutched the fence.

"What was it?"

"It was"—she looked at him and looked away—"it was awful nice."

"Well, what the hell was it?"

"It was a funny kind a flower. It was a flower I bet you never seen before. It was—red, white and blue."

He laughed. "You better go pick it then, Pearly Havla. I ain't got time. Gee'p there!"

But as the horses scrambled at the road she called again, and again he checked them and let the reins go slack.

"You saw what else?"

"A snake."

"You didn't."

"Hope to die I did. Right over there in the woods."

"What kind of snake?"

"I don't know. It was an awful big snake. I bet it musta been six feet long."

She added, watching him watching her grimly, "I think it was a rattlesnake."

Joe made a derisive noise in his throat. He dropped the reins and walked over to her where she teetered with her elbows on her knees and her chin in her hands.

"Pearly Havla," he said into the pale round eyes, "you're an awful little liar. You didn't see a rattler. They ain't been a rattlesnake around here in God knows when. You didn't see a snake at all."

"Honest I did."

The eyes were as candid as the heifer's.

"I bet I can find that snake," she said, "if we go look."

Joe said, roughly, "You get the hell home, Pearly. Your pop oughta give you a good licking."

Pearly's eyes did not change. She did not move her face from her hands. But after a moment, not shifting her gaze from his angry scowl, she told him to go—himself. The word fell from her lips as smoothly as he had heard it fall in barrooms and to him it seemed to stick in the air between them as if she had written it on a fence so that the word and Pearly's mouth and eyes were all one, fixed and wooden. He faced them as if he were facing an impassable fence and after a moment he wheeled about with no word of his own and walked back to the horses and picked up the reins and drove on toward the barn in the distance.

Pearly got down. When he had entered the barn she looked around her at the wheat and the weeds and the deep woods softening in the afternoon glow. Presently she began to saunter along the road to Little Salem, humming tunelessly. She hopscotched once and at last broke into a run and she sobbed as she ran and blubbered all the bad words she could think of.

4

Supper, explained Mrs Purdy, was just a snack and she was putting it on the table early—the meat left over from noon dinner and the honey and preserves already on the clean oilcloth and the string beans and the carrots and the soda biscuits coming up from the kitchen range—so they could get to the Harvest Home in plenty time with her cherry pie and her pound cake and the ham she'd been baking the blessed day, of which they were not to touch a crumb except, perhaps, the cake just to see if it was light enough and goodness knows it ought to be, the eggs she'd put in. Exultantly she dished and declaimed while the two men ate forthwith, having learned the futility of damming the flood until the spring ran dry. When she sat with a panting sigh Joe winked at his father.

"Hear about that fellow over by Frenchtown? Whistled all the time. Got so he couldn't talk for whistling. Now he's in a New York show, just whistling."

Mrs Purdy suspended her morsel of beans.

"I do declare it reminds me of that fellow in the paper—he had the hiccups so bad——"

"This fellow's looking for a helper," interrupted Joe. "Know anybody wants a job in New York?"

Mrs Purdy rested her fork on her plate. She contemplated Joe, on her face swift anxiety.

"What's a fellow like that want a helper for?" said Purdy, chewing.

"To do his talking for him." Joe finished half a biscuit and looked up at his mother, still anxiously watching him. "Thought you might be interested in the job, Ma."

"Joe Purdy, are you talking about going to New York? Because if you are——"

She stopped when he pushed back his chair, and when he got up and took a pot from the stove anxiety struggled with bewilderment.

"Ma," said Joe, "I always claimed you were vaccinated with a phonograph needle and I guess you can't help talking a lot, but I aim to keep you from talking yourself to death." He spooned beans into her plate. "Eat!" he ordered.

"But it ain't good for me! The Hollinses was always too fat!"

"Eat." He put two biscuits with the beans.

"But I will be eating! At the Harvest Home! You know how ev'body——"

"I know how they all eat but you. Eat them carrots too."

"All right. But you ought to be ashamed of yourself, joking an old woman, and, besides, you had me downright scared awhile ago——"

"Eat!"

She ate and so did the two men, and the late glow entered the kitchen, and silence except for the clink of forks and crunch of teeth. Purdy finished first. He sat back in his chair, one foot across his knee. Lit by the glow, his face looked gaunt, its only life the sudden thrust where his tongue worked at a scrag.

Joe said, "I saw Mr Faith today," and knew that his father listened by the little jerk of his foot.

"He said was no cause for you to worry. He said for you to see him if that fellow Buckmeister pestered you."

Purdy's foot jerked again and sound died dryly in his throat.

"Was that his car passed?" asked Mrs Purdy. "I heard a car pass 'bout one o'clock when I was out in back. It was right after

Mr Trimble went up the hill. That Mr Trimble is a nice man. I asked him to the Harvest Home. I said——"

Purdy's foot and chair came down. He rapped out, "What's Jack Faith know about my business?"

Mrs Purdy said, "Now, Lance——"

Joe said, "He was trying to help you; he——"

Purdy swept a nervous hand through the air. "I'll thank him to keep out of my business. What's he know about me? What's he know about farming? Cruising round the county stirring up people against their best interests when he ain't drunk in some barroom. He's a bad influence, a bad influence!"

"Aw, naw he's not, Pop. Mr Faith's a fine fellow."

Purdy made his strangling noise. "A fine fellow, is he? A fine fellow the way he cusses, the way he takes the name of the Lord in vain every time he draws breath and worse! Yes sir, I've heard your fine fellow talk so dirty I'm surprised the Lord didn't strike him dead!"

Joe was silent. Mrs Purdy shook her head, pursed her lips and opened them. "I hear tell they won't renew the licenses of some of those places. Seems they got so many on Twenty-eight——"

"And furthermore"—Purdy shook his finger at them—"if that fellow pokes his nose in my business, I'll order him off my farm. It's still my farm!" His voice shrilled, cracked.

Joe said, "Aw, for God's sake, Pop——"

"Joe!"

"Aw, gee"—he appealed to his mother—"I was just going to tell him Mr Faith said he was too fine a man to let a little squirt like Buckmeister pester him."

Purdy got up. His eyes protruded; his whole arm shook with his finger.

"You too!" he whispered. "You, too, talking thataway!" And suddenly his face went gray-green. He struck a hand to his lips and clopped for the door, but with a mighty effort he turned.

"Still my farm!" he gulped and, gulping, disappeared.

Joe sighed. "Gosh, I didn't mean to start him off——"

"You shouldn'-a mentioned Mr Buckmeister. You know how he worries; you know how the least little thing upsets his indigestion. Now he'll be sick." She panted to her feet and began to clear the table. "All that good food," she mourned, "all that good food!"

"But he worries all the time," said Joe as he helped her. "You can't say anything to Pop might worry him on account he's already worried."

"It's his indigestion. He oughta take a physic."

"He ought not to eat so fast. No wonder he gets sick. He bolts it down 'cause he's worried and then the worry makes him bolt it up again."

"I tell him he oughta see a doctor. Your Uncle Seth was the same way. I've seen your Uncle Seth——"

"And he eats too much," said Joe. "Always talking poor-mouth and how we can't afford a tractor, and then he eats his head off everything we got to sell. Gosh, Ma, if I could just put a tractor on those Heinschmidt fields!"

Mrs Purdy wrapped the cherry pie lovingly in a clean towel.

"Ain't as pretty as our fields."

"They're better soil. That could be an awful pretty farm, Ma."

"I must remember to tell Mr Trimble that. I'll tell him you said so. Maybe Mr Trimble will buy himself a tractor and let you borrow it."

Joe did not answer. Her fingers worked at the last tuck in her bundle, but her eyes were on his back in the open window.

"You better get yourself ready, Joe. We mustn't be late. If you ain't had a bath——"

"I had a bath."

"That's nice. I wouldn't want you smelling sweaty like some of the boys. And it must feel so nice after working all day in the hot fields. Don't you get to worrying, Joe. What's here today 'll be here tomorrow. We been getting along mighty good all these years."

"Aw, Jeez, Ma!" He swung around desperately. "Sometimes I get awful fed up, scrabbling along on the same old land, same old tools, keeping one jump ahead of nothing. Sometimes I wisht it was different. Sometimes I think I oughta get away from here, go out West where the big farms are and they got that swell machinery——"

"Joe!" She came as close to him as her stomach would allow. "Joe, you ain't a-going to New York?"

"Naw-w-w-w."

She adjusted his collar a mite, patting the tie smooth. "You look so nice, Joe. Ain't a nicer looking fellow anywhere. You like it home, don't you?"

"Oh, sure, but——"

"Makes me real proud to have you taking me somewheres. I bet plenty girls will be jealous!"

Joe blushed. "Hell, Ma, I ain't interested——"

He swallowed at his father's entrance. Purdy had doused his head in water. His wet hair clung across his bald spot and he wore a white collar with his clean shirt and his blue Sunday coat. His eyes no longer bulged.

"Better be getting along. Mother, are you ready?"

"I won't be a shake!"

She panted out, untying her apron as she went.

"Son, are you ready? Better see if the car 'll start——"

"It'll start, Pop."

"You can't ever tell. And we don't want to break down——"

"We won't break down."

"Just the same you start her. I'll be closing the windows. Might rain."

His father's voice, jerky, anxious, unintelligible, followed him into the barnyard. Not until he had brought the engine to a drowning thunder could he stop his seething irritation and his self-contempt for having it.

CHAPTER FOUR
VALLEY INN

L AURENCE got the Packard out of the garage and wiped the windshield clean of mashed bugs and the worst dust from the body and the mud from the white-walled tires. He couldn't do much about the stone nicks on the tires or the long scratches in the body's sheen and he mourned a little as he rubbed. Time was when he could part his hair in the fender but the way these country roads ruined a car ought to be a lesson to folks to stay where they belonged, and yet Mr Trimble didn't seem to care if the Packard got busted wide open making haste to trouble every week end. Well, some folks was just naturally crazy. If it was his Packard he'd never drive her off Lenox Avenue unless it was to whirl around the corner to get into Seventh, and if any nigger dared breathe on her he'd lawsuit him. All white folks was crazy anyhow. Down South city-crazy, piling into town till they couldn't get nobody to farm the cotton except niggers they bought out of jail. Up North country-crazy, piling into the country with cars and golf sticks and fishing poles till wasn't enough country left to plant a pea in. Him, he'd take the city, specially up North where colored people had rights. Maybe Mr Trimble believed he felt different, but Mr Trimble would find out different himself come September. He could take the country and Mr Trimble's wages in the summertime, but if Mr Trimble expected him to live away out here when the wind commenced to blow, Mr Trimble was in for a fooling. He'd sass Mr Trimble—that was the way to do it, because you couldn't just quit; you had to get fired in order to get on relief—and he'd hit for Harlem and steam heat and get himself a job and relief both.

Laurence backed and turned and brought the Packard to the gate.

"Heah she is, gen'mens."

Trimble said, "What about your car?"

"I'll leave it," said John Faith, "if I can get your boy to drive it down later on. Then he can pick you up and drive you home. Will you do that, Laurence?"

"Yassuh," said Laurence. "Yas, suh!"

He watched the dust until it settled and the fronds of the disturbed bushes along the lane slept again under the waning sun. At these and the bright Valley he shook his head, much in the manner of De Lawd in *The Green Pastures* surveying His misbegotten world, before he went into the house and closed the windows of his room and on the bed laid him gently down and shut his eyes against the spectacle of Nature's children weaving cobwebs on his ceiling.

Trimble was scarcely out of the lane before he was regretting his unaccountable surrender.

"You should for your own sake," John Faith had said. "Nobody else cares if you bury yourself on the Barrens and put up no-trespassing signs and use shotguns to protect your social isolation. The natives don't care; they think all city people are either snobs or suckers. The naturalized citizens don't care; having been city people, they are more contemptuous of city people than the natives. And the recent aliens like you are too busy warring with the natives and the naturalized to spare a wave for another alien. But you'll miss a lot if you don't see the fun once in a while."

"My dear John," Trimble had protested, "do you realize that is precisely why I came out here—to get away from 'fun'?"

John Faith had wagged his head. "I guess you mean café society. Valley Inn's different. It's like"—he hesitated—"it's like café society and the Rotary Club on a hayride down Tobacco Road. Scrambled eggs American so to speak."

"John, your similes are marvelous! But I don't like café society and I don't like Rotary Clubs. I don't like scrambled eggs. I don't like America either."

"Suit yourself." John Faith had risen. "I just thought you might be a little lonely. Give my regards to the crickets and the fireflies."

It was then Trimble, cursing his own perversity, had said, "Well, I'll come along for one drink," and here he was, deserting his peace in the hour of its acquisition and hating the prospect. "And don't tell me I did it because I'm frustrated," he advised John Faith irritably.

"Okay... but don't put us in the ditch. Better give him the horn and plenty of room."

The Packard, which had been crawling behind a mask of oily smoke and jerking wheels, drew even. Staccato explosions contended with yelps and yells. Trimble had a glimpse of a puckish, suffused face and dogs leaping wildly before he swung back to safety.

"Damn him, he nearly wrecked me. They ought to bar rattletraps like that from the road."

John Faith squinted into the sun's rays, low and blinding now. They were through Little Salem before he spoke.

"Probably drunk," he said. "If not, he will be soon. There's a man knows his own mind. He's been waiting all week for tonight, toiling for it, brooding about it, tasting that first dram of whisky till his tongue curled. Brother, you take your chances when you say 'move over' to a farmer hell bent for the bottle."

"I hope he gets there soon," said Trimble sourly, "with all his animals!"

Faith laughed. "There's only two, the setter and the police dog. That police dog's the meanest in the county. He'd go for you if you looked cross-eyed at his master, and Havla 'd kill the man who touched the dog."

"Havla?"

"Yeah. Lives a couple of farms from you. He went a little nuts when his wife died. Cares more about his dogs than his six kids. When he piles into that car and it starts spitting and shooting and the dogs yowl and he bops them and cusses them you'd think the devil himself was off to town. Here's where we turn."

Trimble, who had been about to ask another question, concentrated on brake and wheel. Like a tired stream glad to toss its burden on the stronger river, the macadam spun into the concrete. The Stop sign dropped behind and Route 28 stretched its smooth twin ribbons along the Valley's floor.

2

When the day man had gone Gunderson hung up his coat and put on his white jacket. Wetting his hair, he bent his knees to bring his face and massive shoulders into the long bar mirror's reflection and combed back the blond morass until it shone like pulled candy. He restored the comb to his pocket and began to arrange the bar to his satisfaction, which never agreed with the day man's.

It was deeply cool and quiet here like a spring in the woods. The beer taps gleamed moist as ferns, ice chilled the air and there was a fragrance of mint and the sharp, clean scent of lemons. From a corner of the taproom, where Mrs Danby entertained her party, murmurs scarcely reached Gunderson. He was wiping the glasses—picking them up and caressing them in and out and carefully setting them down on the damp, dark slab of mahogany—when his wife entered from the kitchen.

She had already changed to her waitress's uniform. Gunderson glanced down the shadowy room, past the empty tables and the stone fireplace and the buck's head and the guns and the hunting prints. Only tops of heads were visible above Mrs Danby's booth. He wiped his palms on the seat of his trousers and girdled his wife. His big hands slowly, caressingly found her flesh under the thin cloth, pressed her breasts hard into his belly. She did not resist while he held her atiptoe, both her hands tight across his spine, their mouths locked.

When he let her go, "Watch out for the boss when you pull that stuff," she said, fixing her hair.

"I'll break him in little pieces," Gunderson said. He slapped her bottom. "Get the hell out of here, Mrs Gunderson."

A man in corduroys and riding boots came through the street door, batting his calves with a crop. He was hatless and tanned and almost as big as Gunderson. Swart hair grew close on his skull, trimly under his thick nose. Where his skin met the neck of his blue sports shirt it was as dark as his face. You knew that he must be dark, hairy all over.

"Hello, Mr Stone," said Gunderson. "How's the big dairy farmer?"

Stone, frowning, leaned on the bar. "Give me a brandy and soda," he said. He tapped his crop while Gunderson made the drink.

"Get your Holsteins okay?" Gunderson said.

Stone lowered the drink, wiped his mustache on the back of his hand and called somebody named McVitty a filthy son of a bitch several times. When Gunderson indicated with his eyes and chin the far booth Stone stopped cursing but did not soften his voice.

"Twenty-eight cows! Twenty-eight cows and a bull! Over five thousand dollars they cost me! And for what? To make baloney for delicatessens! And all because I was ass enough to think one of your damn yokels knew something about livestock!"

Gunderson, who already had heard the story from McVitty, said innocently, "You mean to tell me that whole herd tested bad?"

Stone swallowed, chewed ice. "All but the bull," he said.

Gunderson knew from McVitty that Stone had insisted on going West for his cattle against the dealer's advice. When Stone sent McVitty to inspect the cows McVitty had warned him that he didn't like the way most of them formed up. Stone stubbornly bought the herd and on the tuberculin retest the state of New Jersey had condemned them. It was a plain case, McVitty had told Gunderson and everyone else listening, of a smart aleck out-smarting himself and, in his rage, trying to pass the buck.

Gunderson said now, "So the butcher cut 'em down." He made the familiar, regretful suck of tongue to teeth. "Too bad! One bull won't do you much good on a farm with no cows, will it?"

Stone drained his glass and, while Gunderson refilled it with ice, stared at the bartender with eyes that suddenly reddened. "Look here, Bill," he said, "if that crook thinks he can trick me into selling my place he's crazy. You can take that back to him, see?—you can tell him I'll see him in hell first!"

Gunderson looked up. Blandly he surveyed Stone. Blandly he said, "Me? Are you talking to me? Maybe you'd better tell that to some of your hired help in New York, Mr Stone."

He polished the bar with a damp rag and Stone, after a moment in which his dark skin darkened deeper, poured from the brandy bottle and squirted a siphon. Propped on one elbow, he addressed the taproom.

"No sir," he said, "no sir—that place of mine is too sweet a place to let some yokel grab it for a pigsty. Why, I own two hun-dred of the sweetest acres in northern New Jersey, half pasture, half woodland. Know what I'm going to do? Maybe I got stuck on those cows, maybe dairy farming's not my line, it was just a notion anyway. But there's one thing they can't fool me on." He turned back to Gunderson. "That place of mine has the mak-ings of one of the finest game preserves in the country and"—his voice traveled down the taproom—"nobody can fool me on wild life! Right now I've got a syndicate of rich men in New York ready to come in with me whenever I say the word. We'll make my place a game paradise!"

Gunderson went on polishing the bar.

"Yes sir," said Stone, "a game paradise!"

Meanwhile, in the booth at the far end of the taproom, Rodney Crane expanded for the little lovely one's instruction his formula for the successful novel, punctuating his thesis with small knee prods and an occasional academic grasp of the little lovely one's forearm. She did not seem to mind; her eyes between the blond hinges of her Dutch bob were two blue teacups of admiration … blue teacups … how crisp a metaphor! … his knees joyfully moved in.

"You will also do well, lovely one"—he pontificated—"to give the thing significance. The critics adore significance—of what or which or whither doesn't really matter. In fact the more will o' the wisp the significance the more impressive the work. If you can manage the completely opaque significance of Joyce, yours will be greatness, but I suggest for you, sweet, merely a best seller, for which we shall select significance tangible and in the mode— let us say social significance," driving home his climax with a plump pat.

Across the booth Mrs Danby's smile might have been the benediction of a pleased hostess on house guests agreeably at play instead of an electrode for the murder in her heart. The boredom and impulse which had trapped her, this time, into inviting a literary celebrity to Greenfields long ago had shriveled into nostalgia for a few hearty, unlettered brokers who, if they also drank up one's liquor and tried to seduce one's niece, at least must report to Wall Street on Mondays. Did all authors, alighting in comfortable bedrooms—Mrs Danby asked herself—nestle until they had finished a book? And how naïve to hope that a young girl, no matter how stupid and frivolous, could irritate an aged literary lecher into flight.

"But Bibby," she interrupted, "doesn't intend to write a novel; she's going on the stage, aren't you, Bibby?"

To her aunt's interruption Beatrice Lowe vouchsafed the slow squeeze of her lips and eyes which her mirror and most of undergraduate Princeton approved. She said nothing; it occurred to Mrs Danby that what Beatrice had said since her arrival, if speech had been gin, wouldn't have kept Rodney in rickeys for an afternoon.

"Oh yes she will!" Rodney banged his stirrer imperiously against his glass. "She will write a novel because expression is as necessary to Bibé"—he gave it the full French twist—"as—as— the sun! The lovely one shall write a novel and her uncle Rodney shall help her and it will sell a hundred thousand copies and be bought by the movies for fabulous gold. For it will have significance—social significance!"

"I hate the sun," said Beatrice. "I burn all funny."

"It will," said her adopting uncle, "raise hell with business. There is nothing like raising hell with business to succeed today. Look at Roosevelt, look at Labor, look at Steinbeck. The villain in our novel, my sweet, will be any foul fellow who has a job and can afford an automobile with piston rings that don't leak. He is viciously addicted to work, washing and sanitary toilets. He——"

As graciously as if she were entering into the fun Mrs Danby suggested that Beatrice might not be very familiar with business.

"Doesn't matter in the least," declared the oracle. "The less she knows about business the more savagely and effectively she can attack it. And of course we must have romance. In that department I am sure the lovely one will require no avuncular advice——"

"Mr Crane wants another rickey, Bill," said Mrs Danby, "and I guess I'll break down and try a tom collins. He makes them deliciously, Bibby."

The younger generation once more nonplused her. "Coca-Cola, please," breathed Beatrice and followed the pronouncement with an upward glance and a slow squeeze that caused in

Mrs Danby a catch of sheer panic. They might not drink like their elders, but oh boy!

"And there"—nodded Rodney—"shall we say, goes our hero, the clodpate Apollo!"

"He isn't," protested Mrs Danby. "Bill's almost the nicest guy I know."

Back at the bar, Gunderson gave Stone his change.

"Is that Mrs Russell Danby over there?" said Stone.

"Right."

"Owns the big place just as you come into Madison?"

"Right."

"I've been meaning to meet her ever since I bought out here." As Gunderson made no comment Stone added, "We know a lot of the same people in New York."

"Well," said Gunderson, "we got a rule against pickups in this bar but it don't apply to Mrs Danby. What Mrs Danby does goes, see? And I guess if Mrs Danby wants to meet you—or don't want to—she can handle her social etiquette without no help from me."

With that Gunderson began to mix a tom collins as if he were an acolyte preparing the host while Stone, after another frown and a curt pick at his nose, strolled down the taproom. To the tom collins Gunderson spoke.

"Game preserve! Great god on a mountain, what will they dream up next? They come out here with no more idea what it's all about than a hick hitting town. Asking this, asking that—do pigs bite, can a duck crow?—and every one of 'em already set on some scheme he read in a book or got the low-down from a Broadway farmer. Gonna get rich, gonna beat the local boys at something they learned at the breast. Raising chickens, raising turkeys, raising goats and gimmicks and god love us. And will they take advice? Like Lee took Grant. These yokels don't know nothing, give that big brain from the city a chance. Yokels! Game preserve! They can't fool me on wild life, chum, I shoot

woodchucks and wear tight pants and everything. Hell, if he's
got all that dough he ought to take it down to Jamaica and give it
to the mutuels where he'll have a chance. Me, I don't know why I
tend bar when I could get rich selling left-handed hoe handles to
slickers from Park Avenoo—— Hello, Harve."

The gentleman accompanying him, Harvey Slope announced
to Gunderson, was just coasting along in the capacity of cupbearer. Somewhere, sometime between sunup and sundown
of the night before Slope had been poisoned. He was not sure
whether he had eaten bad food or been poisoned by his enemies.
Since he could not remember eating anything at all his enemies
must have dealt the blow, and Slope suspected that the dastard
was one who for a time had clashed bumpers with him, namely,
that fellow Faith. Whoever the caitiff, Slope had wakened early
that morning in dire pain and had been ill, actually ill.

"The first time," he confided to Gunderson, "the first time in
twenty years I have, to use the classic phrase, flashed my hash."

Gunderson expressing restrained sympathy, Slope ordered
two rye whiskys over his companion's protest.

"I don't care," said Slope, "whether you're not having any or
not, I mean whether you're having any or are—what the hell do
I mean? The point is you're only a cupbearer. Do you know my
cupbearer, Bill? Mr Mayhew—Mr Gunderson!"

Gunderson bowed and Mayhew, who knew Gunderson as
well as the head of the Mayhew Construction Company, the
president of the Community Club and a candidate for county
freeholder knew every voter in Madison, grinned feebly. He was
very miserable. Among other woes, his face hurt, for he had
been grinning that way—grinning and holding it, like a movie
star making a personal appearance—ever since he had unwisely
dropped in on Harvey Slope in the heat of the afternoon and
Slope had insisted on touring all the township bars in the interest,
Slope had declared, of the public. "They are poisoning the public,
Mayhew, and you owe it to your constituents to investigate 'em!"

His constituents, forsooth—oh dear, he was beginning to talk like this fellow!—he could answer to his constituents, but how was he going to answer to Mrs Mayhew?... You see, my dear, Slope's paper is pretty important to me right now with the election coming on and, besides, he's considering building this house... and he made me drink; he absolutely *made* me.... No, it wouldn't do, you really can't expect a waiting wife to nod amiably because, forsooth—oh dear!—her husband has been a cupbearer.

"Where did he get it?" said Gunderson when Slope went to the men's room. "He had a load on last night but Harvey generally sobers up the day after."

Mayhew waved a resigned hand. He was too unhappy for denunciation. "First it was something about a smashup," he said, "and then it was this silly poisoning business. I've had the devil's own time keeping him out of trouble."

Gunderson, shaking his head, started to ask Mayhew whether he had also kept that construction job out of trouble but decided the poor heel was in for enough hell when he reached the doghouse.

"Mrs. Mayhew phoned awhile ago," he said.

Mayhew groaned.

In the booth Mrs Danby had acknowledged Stone's introduction with her Community Club smile and delivered him unvisad to her guests. Immediately Stone inferred enmity all around. He sat down to cure or defy it.

"I've heard of you," he offered Rodney. "Write, don't you?"

The winner of the Pangloss Prize for the best biography of 1931 did not reply to the barbarian who plainly had premeditatively insulted him. He merely blinked rapidly while his lower lip drooped as if it were a third eye pouch. Poor Rodney, thought Mrs Danby, he looks like a child about to cry. She said compassionately, "Mr Crane is the author of *Centaur's Blood*—about

General Sheridan, you know," completing with her postscript the outrage to fame.

Stone brightened. "Sheridan—I've heard of him all right." He slapped the crop and laughed. "He rode too. You know, Mrs Danby, I'm like the Kentuckians, horseflesh and beautiful women are two things they can't fool me on. Do you ride? I find riding the only decent exercise available hereabouts unless one wants to pitch hay with the yokels, God forbid!"

The boor, the swine!—thought Rodney—he knows no more about horses than I do, which is damn little. Damn his eyes, I ought to insult him back but insult would be too good for him. Rodney, Rodney! this is what comes of accepting week-end invitations! One lays oneself open to anything. Stupidity, insults, impossible people. Heat or no heat, I've a good mine to go back to New York. It would serve her right for that dumb crack about The Book. If it wasn't for the little one— —

He started in genuine agony; the little one had stepped on his corn.

"I think it's a fight," she cooed.

Past that swine's nigger kinks and his bore's rasp Rodney observed what, indeed, seemed to be an altercation at the bar.

The little man in rumpled seersucker apparently was forcing a drink on the beanpole in tweeds though he had to reach up like a midget to the mouth of the human skeleton. Bones, ineffectually waving him off, wore a smile that was positively ghastly.

"Stella, forsooth!" Rodney heard the little man shout. "Would you have me die the black death to stop a good wife's tongue? I will call her up and explain you're too drunk to talk but drunk, by heaven, in a noble cause! Drink, Ganymede, drink!"

To Rodney, shuddering, the midget suddenly was the horrid specter of himself. He saw a scuffle and a splatter and the clodpate Apollo bend across the bar and calmly pluck the teetering glass.

"Easy there, Harve," said Gunderson, "or I'll bounce the both of you."

At that moment, through the street door, entered a baseball team followed by two men not in uniform, of whom one might have escaped from the pages of *Esquire* and the other to have been Abraham Lincoln without the beard, or is the historical novel haunting me, thought Rodney.

"John!" screeched the little man and made for Lincoln. "You old son of a gun! Didja hear the news?—I've been poisoned!"

Everyone in the booth had now turned toward the bar.

"There's that real-estate fellow, Faith," said Stone; "he tried to stick me once," when to his surprise Faith began to wave and along with him most of the baseball team.

"Hello!" Mrs Danby was calling. "Hello!—hello!—hello!——"

"Perhaps, my sweet," said Rodney, "our novel should be a romance of the War of 1812, in two volumes——"

He stopped, for Beatrice plainly was looking, if her crimpled eyes could be said to be looking, at the baseball team, and, when he felt for it, he could no longer find her knee.

CHAPTER FIVE
HARVEST HOME

WHEN they were getting into the Ford they saw Mr Trimble's car come out of his lane and disappear toward Little Salem, and Mrs Purdy said she bet he was going to the Harvest Home and wouldn't it be grand if Mr Trimble became interested in the church and maybe gave a contribution and goodness knows they needed it if they were going to keep the minister. She got started on Rev Mr Featherstone then and what a fine man he was and what a fine man Mr Trimble was and how she would just love for them to meet and become good friends. Joe drove silently. What with his mother harping on Trimble and his father saying every time a stone bounced, "Go slow, son, go slow—I wish you wouldn't speed up on curves"—as though a piece of junk like theirs could go thirty if you gave her all she had—and what with catching up with old man Havla just outside of town, he was in a lather the whole way.

He wanted to pass old man Havla, whose junk pile was worse than theirs, but his father wouldn't let him. His father began to gag and get that green look when he honked the horn, so he slowed down to nothing and they ate the dust and the cussing and the dogs' barking till they reached the church. With her mouth full of dust his mother went right on talking and what she said about old man Havla was plenty and what she said about Pearly was mighty mean coming from his mother.

"There's something about that brat," she said, "makes me want to speak sharp to her every time I see her. Makes me want to speak sharp to her," she repeated, "though I don't rightly know what it is and I s'pose it ain't her fault with her poor mother dead and a father like that. I declare," she added petulantly, "I could box her ears!"

Suddenly Joe felt a strange sympathy for Pearly Havla and a wish to stick up for her against his mother, but because he himself only an hour ago could have boxed Pearly Havla's ears and now could not explain why he saw any good in her, he kept his mouth shut and pulled the car onto the grass below the cemetery and dutifully helped unload it.

That fellow Trimble's car was not there, he noticed, but there were several others and he recognized most of them, including the preacher's, which you could be pretty sure to find later than nobody's at a Harvest Home or an oyster supper or anywhere the pot was on the fire. He saw Schaeffers' car and was glad of that because it meant Carl Schaeffer might have come and he would have somebody his own age to talk to even if Carl was dumb as hell and a lousy farmer who would sooner leave a streak of grain a foot wide than replace the broken finger in a reaper.

If Carl was not there, it would be just another of those evenings that seemed to be his luck now whenever the church held a sociable—a bunch of kids and a bunch of old folks and of the few in between not one, somehow, he could swap a dozen words with without feeling that he was a lot younger or a lot older than they were.

Church doings didn't used to be like that. Why, he and Holland Heinschmidt used to have a swell time. They used to get a bunch of kids together and play baseball or foot-and-a-half or a game Holland invented called buckety-buck in which one side was "down" and the other side bestrode their backs with great running leaps and the leader of the side in the saddle called, "Buckety-buck, how many fingers up?" and if the leader of the "down" side guessed the number of fingers held up, that side did the leaping and the riding and the other side was "down." It was a good game because no girls would play it. Then, when the picnic or the supper was ready, all the boys sat together at one table or at the foot of the long table and ate the way they pleased without a lot of bossing of their manners and afterward, if there was a bonfire, they fetched wood for it and roasted corn and potatoes or, if there wasn't, they listened to guitar and banjo or watched the men pitch horseshoes or just fooled around and kidded and practiced spitting at a line till it was time to go and they were so darn tired and full of eats they fell asleep on the way home. Church doings were a lot of fun then.

But now, maybe because Holland got killed, maybe because, like his mother said, young people just didn't go to church nowadays, maybe because the fellow who played the banjo died and the fellow with the guitar moved away and the men didn't pitch horseshoes, they only talked and it was all bitter and anxious and dull talk about government and the war, whatever the reason, he didn't have fun at these things any more. Maybe, he decided as his mother and father went up the path while he delayed, looking at the cars where they were newer models than their car, maybe it was because he himself was not a kid any more.

For the thing itself had not changed. At the top of the slope, on the church porch, the same very old ladies occupied rocking chairs brought by neighbors. One of them was Mrs Fisher. She was ninety-three. She remembered Lincoln and the Civil War and yesterday's temperature and she had not missed a Harvest Home since Joe was a baby. In the basement of the church, he knew, the younger women of thirty and forty and fifty would be setting the tables and opening the baskets and bundles. Three or four of the women would assume charge, trying to shoo the others away, saying, "Really, now, it's no bother—my goodness, now, why don't you just sit and rest yourself?" Among these would be his mother and she would tell them going home exactly who brought what, which cakes were rich and which skimpy, the tasty salads and the gritty ones, the buttered sandwiches and the unbuttered and the spiciest jams and the flattest, though she had eaten scarcely a nibble, and weeks afterward she would recall a certain jar of pickles and out of a clear sky mention its deficiencies, not maliciously but with the calm satisfaction of a lawyer citing the record.

The thing had not changed. The ladies had a gas range instead of a wood stove to heat up the meats and soups and pots of beans and cook the oysters for the oyster suppers; they brought the cold lemonade and the cold tea in thermoses. But the ladies were the same and so were their ways. And so were the men's. They would join the ladies when all was prepared; they would eat the blessed food with them and with them, when the tables were cleared and the dishes washed and stored in the cars, sit and chat, the husbands sitting patiently, mostly letting the wives do the talking except when the tale went so wrong they couldn't stand it and had to break in and put it on the right track and perhaps finish the tale as it should be finished or race against the wife to reach the finish first. Meantime, until the ladies called them, the men collected and did not pitch horseshoes but talked and laughed a little.

The younger women and the younger men, they who were boys and girls yet no longer children, patterned their behavior on their elders'. Girls flocked to girls and boys to boys; seldom did the groups exchange more than greetings; rarely did one member single out one other from the opposite group, and what meeting of glance and smile and word befell did so when two young joined the old. And so it was even with the very young.

Joe could see a scattering of these in the lot where the canning factory once stood. Small boys ran violently; their voices shrilled in triumph and despair. He watched a moment, but the game was one he did not know and, speaking quickly to the old ladies, he went on around the church to the oak grove in the rear.

He looked for Carl Schaeffer and could not find him among the handful of youths at the edge of the grove. He waved and entered the basement and spoke to Mrs Schaeffer. Carl, she said, had gone off somewhere in his new car, the Chrysler he'd picked up last week and got such a good trade-in on. He'd said maybe he'd get to the Harvest Home later but you never could tell about Carl, especially since he got the Chrysler, he was that wild and so crazy for the rollerskating. Looking up at him, her pink face woeful yet quizzical, she said, "Ach, that Carl! He iss a fine boy but not so fine as you, Cho. Always I have said it, there is none handsomer than Cho, but Cho is a home boy too."

That pleased yet nettled him and he got away from her as fast as he could and from all those women. In the grove he passed Eunice Littleton and the Olafson girls and some others he didn't know. Eunice called, "When are you coming to see me, Joe?" but he just grinned and waved and hurried his step. He wanted no part of Eunice Littleton and her crowd with the airs they'd put on since they'd grown up. Because he used to tease her with bugs and spiders she thought she could tease him now. Hell, he'd show her he was no kid any more.

The boys were all younger than he, a bunch still in high school. They were talking about the new rink at Gellerstown. Fred Romerley said it was a honey. He said on Saturday nights they had a swing band and dance contests for the best dancers on skates and stayed open till two and three o'clock Sunday morning and what went on was nobody's business. He said there was a bowling alley and bar attached to the rink and you couldn't go into the bar from the rink but you could from the bowling alley and if you were smart about where you parked your car you could slip out beer to the girl friend or anything else.

"Wha' do you mean, anything else?" said George Monski. Everybody yelled. George Monski laughed so hard he rolled on the grass. But Fred Romerley did not laugh. He looked scornful. He said hell, he didn't go in for that back-seat stuff. He said that was for kids. He said if he had something hot he took it to Tourists' Rest, where you got a cabin and everything for a buck.

And if he didn't roll his own, he said, he went there anyhow and got one on the house for another buck. They were usually pretty hot stuff too. Last week at Tourists' Rest he had him a girl from Portland, Oregon.

"Any of you fellows want to match for a cigar?" said Joe. Fred said sure, he'd match him and started to fumble for a coin, but he went ahead telling them about the girl from Portland, Oregon, while he drew out the quarter and didn't toss when Joe tossed, so Joe put his own coin back and listened with the rest of them. Then Toad Norton told about a girl from Denver, Colorado, who thumbed him one time on 28 and by the time Toad got through Fred had put his coin back.

"Well, gentlemen," said George Monski, "shall we start talking about nooky now or wait till the train starts?" and everybody laughed but Joe, who didn't see what was so funny. He guessed he didn't keep up with things good. He said to Stan Titcomb, who stood next to him, "Any rain up your way, Stan? Our corn's beginning to curl up."

"You'll have to ask the old man—that's his department," Stan said and turned to Fred Romerley, who was talking again. So Joe listened. Not, he thought, because I give a damn what kids say. He can lay all the women he wants to for all of me. And it ain't because it's dirty that I don't care; I just ain't interested, I just ain't interested.

He began to think about the old Heinschmidt farm—he might plant wheat this fall in the top field if Trimble didn't care and the chances were Trimble didn't know wheat from oats—when he became aware that they had all stopped talking and were looking at him and that Fred Romerley, who had spoken last, was grinning.

"Wha'd you say, Fred?" he asked.

"Any nooky up your way, Joe?" said Fred Romerley. "Case mine begins to curl up."

George Monski rolled on the grass again. The others yelled.

"I know where he's got nooky," said Stan Titcomb, "and not so many farms from his. Course it's kinda young corn!"

"Yeah," said Fred Romerley, "I know about that. But you fool around with that, pal, and you'll get a bullet up your ass."

"I ain't afraid of her old man."

"You're afraid of his dog then."

"Oh, I dunno. That dog don't stop you, does it, Joe?"

They all watched him, not grinning now, curiously, wisely, like a court waiting for a verdict yet sitting in judgment as well. He was getting mad but he said, trying to grin too, "I don't brag about my crop till I'm done reaping."

They howled. George Monski rolled on the grass and got up and rolled again. They punched Fred Romerley. Even Fred laughed and clapped Joe's shoulder and called him a cozy apple. But all the time they were hailing him and later, still listening to them and finally trooping with them toward the church—calling, "When do we eat?" mocking the girls' answers, "Come and get it!"—all the time he hated them.

He hated them only a little for the lie he had told. Pearly Havla, after all, was anybody's meat and a man cannot deny his manhood. He hated them more for his need to lie, for the thing they were and the thing they did to him, making him a liar and a coward and one of them whose ways were not his ways. His hatred was like his hatred of his father, churned out of his own self-contempt and foaming blindly on all around him.

Down the long room he saw his father's face, gray-green, anxious, peering, and he thought, that is the way you peer at everything, your food, your farming, your future, like a hound-dog snarling but afraid of a kick; damn you, don't peer at me.

And he saw his mother's face, signaling as if she implored him to please wash his hands and be gentle with his father and not run away out West, and he thought, Jesus, is this the way it is always to be, washing and women and being nice to kids and jackasses because they belong to the same church or the same family or the same town?

And he looked at the other faces, old Mrs Fisher, who was here when he was born and would probably be here when he died, Eunice Littleton and the girls of Little Salem he had teased in pigtails and could no longer tease nor yet escape in their fluffed maturity. Fred Romerley's face and Toad Norton's and George Monski's and the face of the preacher, which reminded him, when the preacher beamed at the sisters, of Fred Romerley's face telling about the girl from Portland, Oregon.

They were faces he had known all his life; they were the faces of his own blood, his own people, yet none of them was pleasing or even tolerable. This morning he had been happy in sight of nothing but a cock pheasant soaring out of the corn. For God's sake, what was the matter with him? For God's sake, what did he want?

"And now, dearly beloved, let us bow our heads and give thanks to the gracious Lord, who has so bountifully blessed us tonight," said Rev Featherstone.

In humiliation and arrogance and loneliness for what, he could not say, only that it was far likelier to be found under a clean and windy sky than in the basement of Little Salem Church, Joe Purdy bowed his head.

2

Selena came out on the porch and counted three more cars and took note that the old ladies had disappeared. Everybody, then, would be in the basement, eating. She went upstairs and put on a hat and brought down the suitcase and set it in the store just inside the screen door. On the porch she faced away from the church, shading with one hand the eyes already shaded by her hat. Long after the sun had set, its luster stayed on houses and tracks and macadam. Nothing moved in this brightness. For the first time since early afternoon uncertainty ruffled the inflexible lines about her mouth.

They had been there, tight as the fist she shook at Emil and the Ford, from the moment she dropped her arm and entered the house. Unhesitating, she had gone up to the bedroom and, mounting a chair, reached down the suitcase. Dust covered it. But when she had wiped it and flung it open the lining seemed as crisp as new. She turned a flap and a sheet of paper slid from the fold and she picked it up. Reading it—an advertisement for Dr Blodgett's Peptones—and standing there holding it, frowning at the suitcase, she could think of only three times the suitcase had been used; her honeymoon, a visit to her sister in South Orange the year after she was married and Emil's trip to Trenton to see the creditors after his father's death. That was the last time and that was eight years ago. Eight years ... her lip curled as she balled the paper into a wad and tossed it into a corner. Thereafter, despite the tinkle of the bell below which meant someone was in the store and she must go down, she had worked steadily through all her closets and bureau drawers, cramming the suitcase until only by sitting on the lid could she close and lock it.

When she had done, the bedroom held her. There was something in its shabby desolation that was unendurably disreputable. She went about neating the tumbled drawers, putting away garments she had discarded, even dusting. The wad of paper in the corner halted her. She smoothed it out and pinned it to Emil's pillow. Didn't people always leave notes when they went away? There ... that was her note! But almost immediately she tore the paper from the pin in a gust of revulsion.

She began to shake, crumpling and recrumpling the scrap in her hand, and this was anger that shook her and drove the nails into her flesh and constricted her throat and beat at the back of her eyes. It was anger so fiercely irresistible that she would have cried out in joy had Emil entered to receive her physical attack. It was a great anger, born of no single seed but a myriad, coagulating and bursting in an avalanche of contempt the stronger for the years she had curbed it and no lesser for the realization that nothing concerned in it but was petty and mean and cheap and that nothing she could do—no word, no blow, no parting sneer—could avenge her for all Emil had done and all that he had failed to do.

Still in the grip of this unreasoning and despairing fury, yet not crying out or permitting it to hasten her a step, she quit the bedroom for the kitchen. There she washed and dried every dish, arranging them neatly on their shelves and mopping the floor and removing the garbage to the backyard.

Not until she had changed the fly ribbons for fresh ones and found no spot to scour did the ferment in her wane to a dull, sullen smolder. In the bathroom she washed all over with a cold cloth and put on her best dress; it was then she disposed the suitcase and went out to the road.

The bright solitude that challenged her now trembled with no mirages. Her mind felt wrung, dulled as her rage. She tried to think what she should do if Emil did not return soon with the Ford. She had not thought of this before; she had thought only that at last and at once she must go. Wherever she went would be better than here; whatever befell no worse. And of course she would go in the Ford. But—there was no Ford. My God, was she to be licked—climb the stairs, unpack the suitcase—by a peewee husband and a Ford?

Across the narrow, dusty stretch stood a dozen cars. Their idle motors taunted her; what prevented her from riding off in any one of them? Yet this she could not do without a by-your-leave, if refusal to do it meant Emil for eternity. A clatter of dishes rose, a murmur of voices from the white church fading into the white twilight. She shrugged and went inside the store.

The old man slept in his chair in front of the radio, so deflated, so inert that all of him seemed to have died save the breath sputtering feebly where his teeth hung in their sockets. When he was awake he was forever sucking back the plate, and she prickled with an impatient desire to straighten it now. But she let him be, thinking only when he wakes and calls I will not be here. At least, she thought, he can have his rumpus. She replaced the electric plug she had removed earlier.

She was standing in front of the kitchen mirror, pressing a tiny pimple in her cheek and debating whether to squeeze it, when she heard the bell in the store tinkle and the screen door close.

3

Joe said, "How do, Mrs Gillibo?" and, seeing Selena's hat, "Were you going out? I just want a cigar."

She preceded him to the shelf where the cigars were kept and, when he named his brand, offered the box. Joe selected two.

"I'm afraid——" Selena said to the dollar bill. She went around the counter to the cash drawer, knowing it was empty.

"Wait a minute," she said. Her purse lay in the other room.

"If you want to put it on the bill, Mrs Gillibo——"

"No—I have it—if you don't mind waiting——"

"Sure—that's all right."

You'd bet it was all right, Mrs Gillibo, if you knew what it's like over there and how fed up I am. It don't mean anything to you, but I was mighty glad to come over here. Anything to slip out for a minute, to get away from that crowd. I dunno why, but they get my goat. Shucks, it's at least quiet over here. For a while, when they were all jabbering, I got so fed up I started to leave in the middle of the chicken. I got to thinking this is what New York's like all the time, and then I thought, hell, Little Salem's getting just as bad; it's getting so you can't find quiet except in a cornfield, and even then some fellow's liable to come along smacking at bees. It's all right, Mrs Gillibo, you take your time. You don't know it, but I'm taking mine.

Joe bit and lit a cigar, the good smoke saturating his nostrils, curling into the good quiet. On the other side of the curtain, the purse in her hand, Selena hesitated.

The purse held—besides thirty-two dollars in bills—much silver, the quarters, dimes and nickels demanded and wrested and hidden from Emil in the long mercenary combat of the years, a struggle she had come almost to enjoy, the satisfaction of smoking out his little hordes, the pleasure of concealing hers past his finding. She did not halt in any realization that this was the last money in the house, nor to count it, for she knew what was there to the penny. She hesitated in sudden speculation on quite another notion.

Since he was a small boy she had known Joe Purdy as one of a battalion of children forever filing in and out of the store on family errands or to make small purchases of sweets and soda for themselves. While they spoke politely, they always gazed out of their inscrutable children's eyes as if they feared or judged her, she never could tell which, and she, with her indifference hardening in the conviction that their manner but reflected some attitude of their parents, waited on them with scant attention even to their identity. There were children who grew up or moved away and others who sickened and died and one, she recalled, who was killed by lightning. But there was none she warmed to, for none crossed the gap that separated her from Little Salem and that seemed, in the case of the children, to be the wider for their solemn eyes.

Joe Purdy's eyes were evasive rather than solemn; they would be blue, she guessed, if they were still the color of his small boy's eyes. But of this detail she could not be sure, since she could not remember Joe Purdy looking at her in so long or she actually looking at Joe Purdy. He was a tinkle of a bell, a monosyllable, a rough thumb on a greenback, and that was all he was; he was the child who did not die or go away. But he was also, at this moment, the boss of a Ford.

Selena entered briskly.

"Here you are, Joe—sorry to keep you waiting——"

"That's all right, Mrs Gillibo." She paused in front of him, opening her purse on the counter.

Nightshade had come into the quiet. Selena reached up and pulled the suspended cord and light spilled down her bare arm onto the heap of coins.

"—and seventy, seventy-five, eighty—right?"

On her raised head the light beat past the hatbrim, tipping the nose and the chin tilted under her smile. Caught, Joe smiled back. He had not been looking at his change.

"That's right, ma'am. Thank you. I—I just wanted a cigar."

He seemed to be apologizing for not buying something more, and she, while she schemed swiftly, yet sensed his diffidence and the fact that he had not at once pocketed the money but instead put his cigar to his mouth and then took it away and presently put it back. Smoke sifted through the light.

"Mind if I smoke?"

She laughed. "Much good it would do me if I did."

"Why, sure—I'd stop—cigars are kind of strong."

His eyes were blue. They were blue like May sky. She began to laugh again, slowly, easily.

"Imagine you smoking cigars! It seems like just the other day I was selling you candy—just the other day——"

Joe said, puffing, "I been smoking cigars the last five years. You must know that, Mrs Gillibo; you sold me enough."

"So I have, come to think about it."

"Yeah." After a moment, "Yeah," he repeated, and puffed, and the blue smoke lay quiet between them in the strong light.

Excuse me, Mrs Gillibo—you will excuse me, won't you—for smoking and for not buying anything else and for sticking around here and not saying much. I never could say much, Mrs Gillibo; you ought to know that the times I been in here, but then I never heard you say much either so I guess we're even. I could say plenty now, if I knew how to say it, but it would all be stuff about me and how I feel about things and nobody wants to hear that. But if you don't mind, Mrs Gillibo, I'd like to stay a minute; it's quiet here and it's peaceful and I don't want to go back over there.

She said, "Joe——?"

"Yeah."

"Were you at the Harvest Home?"

"Yeah. Why?"

She did not go on. It was becoming plain to her that he was standing there because he did not want to leave. Something was holding him; something was eating on him, and though she hadn't the remotest idea or concern for what it was, the fact that he lingered of his own will suited hers. At any other time she might have asked him to take her to Madison and the bus stop without a second thought, but the import of that step tonight made her falter and seek an excuse. And she was busily considering what her excuse should be when, suddenly, it was he who went on.

He said, the words rushing out of him, "Sure, I was to the Harvest Home and I don't know what got the matter with me but I couldn't stand it any more; I just couldn't stand it; I had to get out and go somewhere and that's why I come over here. I guess I been to a million of 'em and I don't think I ever did like 'em but I never did feel quite as bad as this time and—and restless—and right now I wish to God I wasn't going back!"

He stopped after the longest speech of his life in amazement at making it and a muddle over why he did and embarrassment that he had. Yet he continued to face her desperately, as if in Mrs Gillibo's eternal composure, the smooth skin, the neat hair, the level look that from childhood had unalterably met him and always a little awed him, he might find the secret and the cure of his unhappiness. Suddenly Selena put out her hand and patted his and it came to him, through his hot confusion, that she, alone in Little Salem, understood his trouble.

"Did—did you ever feel that way, Mrs Gillibo?"

But Selena, for her part, had scarcely listened. She had patted a child. Oh, he was mad; oh, he was piqued as a child at something or somebody who had hurt him. And it was the Harvest Home, was it? Shucks, she could have told him these ten years that crowd didn't matter.

She leaned across the counter, smiling, and sympathy and kindness broke through her imperturbability. For it was not what he said, it was the way he said it—wrought up, appealing so fiercely, ripe for her agreement—that cut away necessity for invention.

"Look," she said, "if that's the way you feel—look, I've got to go to Madison and Emil's got the Ford—do you want to run me over?—we'll talk about it on the way."

"Why, sure," he said, "sure."

Above his sunburned cheekbones the eyes puckered, blue, a little bewildered, but acquiescent to her wish. He's a good-looking kid, she thought.

In the next instant she had caught her breath. That was a car.

CHAPTER SIX
COCKTAIL TIME

AND NOW in the taproom of the Valley Inn and the bar that had been like a cool spring in a murmuring glade voices rose; booths and tables began to fill; the bar banked up with drinkers; someone started the nickelodeon, and a gluey contralto reiterated through the hubbub her yearning for a bluebird. Mr Felixio beamed from the kitchen. To others the scene might be gay or gross; to Felixio, in his chef's cap almost as tall as his diminutive body, it was holiday trade to his soul's content and mucho deposit tomorrow in the Banco di Romano. He shouted cordial salute to the customers and to Gunderson in a quick bark, "No drink on house!"

"Go cut yourself a piece of throat," said Gunderson to the swinging doors and topped his beers. "I'll break that runt in little pieces someday," he assured the company.

The baseball team grinned. They joked Gunderson. They joked each other. They joked victory and defeat and hot weather and the Fourth of July and they eyed, as one man, Beatrice in the far booth.

Mrs Danby's little party had increased. Besides Stone, possessively mounting guard, Faith and Trimble had approached and, stubborn at Faith's heels, Slope, denouncing and lamenting. The editor's power for hullabaloo, extraordinary in so small a man, grew as attention to him wandered. Rodney Crane was goggling, Stone hostile, Beatrice focusing on distance; Faith, taking Trimble's arm, had turned his back; it was as though, by unanimous consent, they were treating his outcries as of no more consequence than his size. Slope settled on his heels and ululated.

"You might," Mrs Danby was saying, "sit down if you can find room."

This tall man's hand she was holding, she was thinking through those dreadful sounds, once before had gripped hers fast, as together they surveyed from her living-room couch the shambles of the party, the spilled ash trays and the dregs of drinks, the servants long ago dismissed and every other guest gone. He had said a great deal that night and it had seemed terribly important and moving, for she was not entirely sober either and she did not know him very well, but what he said she could never afterward satisfactorily recall except that he thought of her in rather a breath-taking way and stars and zinnias were mixed up in it. Obviously sex was not. On this, next day, she had pondered, thinking sardonically, am I wanting at my age to be a fascinating bitch? No, she decided, but I like that man, and afterward, whenever Danby and the brokers said he was a Communist and only used real estate as a blind to get around and incite the farmers, she always championed John Faith.

"This is my niece, Beatrice Lowe," she said, "and I think you know the others. Bibby, this is Mr Faith and back there—the calliope—Mr Slope—Harvey, don't you want to meet my niece?"

Ululation ceased before Gunderson, advancing, reached the booth. The bur on Faith's coattails detached itself, lunged forward, almost upsetting Faith's companion, checked itself abruptly against Stone's knees and with owlish eyes froze the beginning of Bibby's smile. Everybody waited apprehensively for it to speak.

It said, "Evelyn Nesbit!"

Perplexed silence received this remark.

Into the lull Rodney dropped a grace note. He had been experimenting with vision over his spectacles and finding the blear, if anything, more daunting than clarity. Never, not even in Hollywood, Rodney concluded, had he surveyed in one room so many revolting individuals. Suddenly, out of nowhere, they had come boiling like maggots; trampling troglodytes, red faced, huge *Ms* on their chests; a gnome whistling like a steam shovel, a white linen zombi and tall Beelzebub himself fixing him with evil-blue, bloodshot eye. If he screamed, they might vanish; they often did in nightmares. On the other hand, they might not.

Rodney's discretion, grappling with his alcohol, prevailed. He raised his glass to the devil. He said, "Cheerio!"

The devil remarked, "Back up, Harve, you're scaring the child. She's not used to your magnetic eye."

"I don't mind, really I don't," said Beatrice.

"But I do, sometimes he scares me. It's all right, Bill. I'll handle him." Faith plumped the editor into a chair so hard that his hair shook. "Besides, he's in the way. I want to introduce my friend Trimble. Mrs Danby, this is the hermit of Little Salem."

Well, he was in for it now. Laurence might not call for him for hours and while of course he could rightabout-face and march out of Valley Inn and drive back up the Barrens and send Laurence down with Faith's car, it simply wasn't the sort of thing one could decently do. He might as well make the best of it, bow and scrape—ah, yes, the author, how do you do—Stone?—ah, yes, I'm sure we've met in town—how do you do—how do you do— and be agreeable to this Mrs Danby, who, if nothing else, looked smart. "Thank you," he said as she moved over in the booth.

Conversation at once became both general and particular, as inevitably it does in barrooms, with talk between two chopped by speech from all, fragments of remarks hopping into vagrant ears and the whole, like hash under ketchup, spattered by the contralto's nostalgia for ornithology.

"Beautiful, you oughta be in handcuffs——"

"Shut up, Harve!"

"But I don't mind him, really I don't."

"But he's drunk—he's a nuisance when he's drunk."

"You mean my cupbearer's drunk. He's getting drunk for me. Where is my cupbearer?"

"Miss Lowe, is he annoying you?" This from Stone, stoutly resisting Slope's unconscious march on his boots.

"But of course not, really he's not!"

"Harve's just a romantic," Faith explained. "This cupbearer business. Probably goes back to the Knickerbocker Bar. You remember the picture? Old King Cole?—and the bowl, you know."

Under the clatter Trimble tried to be at ease. He apologized for intruding. If John Faith hadn't insisted, he never would have come. As a matter of fact he rather enjoyed being a hermit. That's why he bought a country place.

"I know—that's why we all did." Mrs Danby's smile was rueful. "And at first it is rather wonderful. But it's amazing how soon you're dissatisfied, how you want town or—this."

"I think I shall stay satisfied," said Trimble.

"I hope so. So many don't. They buy farms and sell them and come and go, almost like tenants in New York on the first of October. You see, I've watched it happen for years."

"But you are satisfied?"

Mrs. Danby fished for the cherry in her collins. "Don't take me as evidence—I'm one of those awful hostesses who longs all week for guests and by Sunday night prays for their departure. I don't know what I want. Ask Mr Faith—he says I'm frustrated."

Yes, take her, brooded Rodney through the icy heeltap of his rickey—take her and pigeonhole her, Case History X-4, the she-drone, barren, shallow, lazy and bored to death, playing at Lady Bountiful while she feeds her emptiness the brains and talents of her grateful victims; parasite, succuba, tick; Madam Mantis and lo the poor author! Lo the poor author—he perceives her, pigeonholes her, pins her in his book of specimens. But what profiteth it an author to gain copy if, bogged among the bourgeois, he loseth his soul?—Rodney, Rodney! you are getting drunk; stop cerebrating and look to the niece.

The niece at the moment began, "But really——" when Slope struck the table a feeble blow.

"Katherine Hepburn!" he shouted.

The arrival of the waitress relieved a general tension. Everybody ignored Slope and ordered drinks.

Jammed into a corner of the bar, Allison Mayhew recklessly sipped. It was his second highball here, to say nothing of its predecessors, but he was tasting it almost without a qualm. The fat, he had told himself, was in the fire and he might as well be hung for a sheep as a lamb. After what he had been through with Slope he really needed a quiet little drink. Besides, these were, indeed, his constituents; he must be one of the boys. He ordered Gunderson to set 'em up again. He lifted his arm. Here's looking at you, Allie; good luck, fellows! (And nuts to you, Mrs Mayhew; forgive me, dear, I couldn't help it.)

Doc McKasker, at his elbow, went right on talking and he himself went on smiling and occasionally nodding. That was all he had to do, nod and smile and sip. What Doc McKasker said didn't matter or whether he answered Doc McKasker; all that mattered was to keep sipping until that other voice at his elbow thinned, retreated and at least reproached and menaced him no more.

"I don't mean you, Allie," Doc McKasker said. "I know you and I know I can trust you. If you come to me any time without a prescription and said, 'Listen, Doc, I need this stuff bad, I got sickness at my house and I got to have it,' why, I'd sell it to you, see; I don't care what the law says. You wouldn't even have to explain; I'd let you have it because I'd know it wouldn't go no further than between you and I. But there's some people in this town, and I don't have to mention names, they'd beg me on their bended knees to break the law, and the minute I did quick as a flash they'd report me and get my license took away and close my store and put me in jail out of sheer meanness.

"Out of sheer meanness!" repeated Doc McKasker and Mayhew nodded and smiled sympathetically as the bar brightened and all beyond it dimmed.

"Yes sir," said Doc McKasker, "when I use my own judgment that's my own business and I don't tell it and those I trust don't tell it. So why should I tell my business to a fellow I don't even know right well and a fellow who ain't, in a manner of speaking, got business with me? Like I was telling you, this fellow didn't come in to buy; he come in to pick me. 'You know my wife?' he says. 'Why,' I says, 'I believe I do.' He says, 'Have you seen her lately?' and I says, politely, 'She ain't been in today, sir.' He gave me a look, that funny look he was always giving folks when he was living in Madison—I ain't calling his name, because, like I said, I don't tell other folks' business and I trust my friends not to tell mine, but you'd remember that look of his if I mentioned him—he gave me that look, like he suspected I was hiding something from him or putting something over him, and he said, 'I don't mean today; I mean any time lately; have you seen her?' he said, quick and sharplike."

Doc McKasker drained his beer and motioned to Gunderson. The bartender drew the glass full. "And a drink for Mr Mayhew," said Doc McKasker.

Holding the cold and foaming glass, Doc McKasker shook his head in mystery at this fool world. "And me itching to get away to the ball game," he said. "So I think back and I tell him, as polite and honest as I could, 'Why, sure,' I says, 'I seen your wife one day but it must have been at least a week ago. She was standing right outside there looking in the window,' I says; 'I remember it because she stood there looking for quite a spell but she never come in. That's why I remember it,' I says to him, 'because she never come in and, after all, Mister—and I called his name—we like folks to come in the store and, when they do come in, we like 'em to buy something!' and I gave him a wink so he'd understand that maybe I was joking but maybe I wasn't."

On and on, that was all that mattered, an endless voice requiring no answer or remark. Stella's voice was muted now, lost in the rising chorus. Sigrid, the waitress, said excuse me at Mayhew's left and he moved closer to McKasker while she leaned across the bar and added her distraction to the rest.

"Two tom collins, two ryes, one brandy and soda, one gin rickey and a Coca-Cola. Ya got that?"

"I got it." Gunderson's glance roughed her swiftly, fondly above the beertops; Sigrid smacked her gum at the baseball team; Felixio bobbed out and into the kitchen, and the doleful contralto surrendered to a fast foxtrot. Havla entered through the street door with his two dogs.

He was a scrawny, brittle little man, puckered of face, halt of step. The yoke of ages shadowed him and the catastrophes of all weathers. His hat hung crushed on his ears, his pants abject at his bowed knees. Not a glimmer showed valor for a tilt at earth or man or the bottle. He quailed as he came into the light. The red setter, like its master, cowered head to the floor, sad eyes and rash tail beseeching the world's forgiveness. The huge "police" dog defied whatever came. At its rumble Havla turned and struck the bared fangs and dragged the setter onward by its worn leash.

"Please, missy"—he paused by Sigrid—"whisky, please?"

The waitress did not miss a beat in the champ of her jaws as she recognized her man. "Pint of Granddad, wrap it up!" she called. But Gunderson went on mixing drinks.

Havla waited, holding the big dog by a hand thrust under its collar, the setter shivering against his feet. Sigrid called again, "Ya got that pint of Granddad?"

Gunderson came out from behind the bar, small one instant as he ducked under the counter, towering his full height the next.

"Beat it," he said.

Havla's puckered face beseeched him. "Whisky, please?" A hand fumbled in the vest. "I pay, Mister."

"Beat it," said Gunderson.

"I thought," said the waitress, "if he got his pint——"

"I told him to beat it." Gunderson was calmly inexorable.

The little man proffered a wrinkled bill. The taproom had gone still except for the foxtrot. The lineup at the bar eyed Havla, eyed Gunderson. Somebody in a booth said "shhh" and the setter's whimper pierced the music.

Felixio slammed out of the kitchen. He barked, "What you do, Gunderson?" The bartender said "Oh, for Cri'sake" to nobody. Felixio bounced under the bar; he came up bristling like a gamecock against leviathon.

"What you say, hah? What you tell him, hah?"

Gunderson, brick red, did not answer.

"So!" crowed Felixio. "So!" He strutted from Gunderson to Havla. "Who is boss here, hah?" He whirled as if to catch the bartender with a knife. "We shall see!" Cautiously, an eye on the dogs, he patted Havla's arm. "It is whisky you want, hah? Okay! I am the boss!"

Gunderson put his back to them. He went under the bar.

Grinning, the lineup relaxed, watching one little man escort the other little man to a table.

"What got into him, Bill?" asked a ballplayer. "He generally throws out bums on their ear."

"I notice he ain't pattin' them dogs," said another.

Gunderson apostrophized his bottles. "Runts—great god on a mountain, what wouldn't I give to exterminate 'em! You can't dodge 'em, you can't sock 'em and God knows you can't tell 'em anything. I'd sooner have a bar fulla wildcats than a bar fulla runts, and the littler they come the meaner they are. It looks like the Lord made up in meanness what he shaved 'em in build. If a runt spots a feller a size more 'n he is he's gotta cut down that feller or die trying. Someday I'm gonna catch me a messa runts and if anybody cracks about a big bully——Sigrid, take him this bottle before I break him in little pieces."

"But I don't understand." Mrs Danby spoke to Trimble but she looked at Faith. "Bill is always so nice. It's usually Mr Felixio that's rude. I wonder who the little man is."

"I think," said Trimble, "his name is Havla."

John Faith abandoned Slope to his fascinations, limited at the moment to Beatrice's way with her straw, and leaned toward them. "You couldn't understand," he said, "because you're native born and take America for granted. Felixio doesn't. He's been in America only fifteen years and it chronically overwhelms him. Life, liberty, the pursuit of happiness and all the rest. He's got to appreciate it. If he were a gangster he'd go out and shoot a few cops. But being a decent, thrifty citizen, he takes it out on the help and the customers. 'I am the boss—let freedom ring'—you get it?"

"No, I don't," said Trimble. "It sounds——"

Rodney bellowed between them. "Decent, thrifty, bah! Russian organizers, Chinese laborers, Italian racketeers, French movie prostitutes, English lecturers! Pilfering the American pocketbook—that's all freedom means to them—dollars! And when they get all they can grab they scamper back to lord it in their own bankrupt countries and thumb their noses at the United States!"

"In a way you're right," agreed Faith.

"Of course I'm right!"

"But in a way you're wrong. Havla's had more hard luck and done more hard work than Daniel Boone. I'm sorry for him."

"Is that why Mr Felixio likes him?" said Mrs Danby. "He's sorry for him?"

"Oh no," said Faith. "Felixio——"

"Bah!" exploded Rodney. "Nobody's sorry for him except sentimentalists. We didn't ask 'em over here; we didn't——"

"Please, Rodney, he's telling me something."

"But maybe Mr Crane is right," said John Faith. "I was about to say that Felixio actually hates Havla because Havla's an Austrian, the northern Italian's natural enemy. That's why Felixio's nice to him—and why the Golden Rule works, I suppose. Love your enemies, the poor mugs."

"How terribly confusing!"

"God created woman—and boredom did indeed cease from that moment," quoted Rodney sarcastically into space.

"You see," said John Faith, "it's like that fellow who pretended to be a Romanoff and became the pet of New York. He was as Jewish as his benefactors, but they got a kick out of patronizing the mere czarist name."

Mrs Danby shook her head. "No," she said, "no—it's all mad."

"Exactly." Trimble got it out at last. "It sounds lunatic."

"But of course," agreed Faith. "Whoever said the world was sane? I wouldn't be surprised to learn that everybody here was a patient, let out for the evening in charge, without their knowing it, of Gunderson. Me—you—Felixio—Havla—Mr Crane there—all nuts."

Rodney, opening his mouth to retort, lost to Stone.

"Your friend," announced Stone crossly, "has gone to sleep."

Slope had indeed—his eyes closed, his mouth open, his head on his hand and this hand pinning Beatrice's to the table. His rumpled hair gave him a startling cherubic look. All gazed at the phenomenon.

Faith got up. "Harve——"

"I don't mind, really——"

"Don't wake him," begged Mrs Danby.

But Faith was shaking the editor's shoulder. "Harve!" he called. "Harve—get up!"

Rodney became aware that the little lovely one had turned to him. Her smile was dazzling. "You——" she breathed and vanished. For several seconds he sat in golden mist. Not until Faith began to haul Slope to his feet did it dawn on Rodney that his hand, not Beatrice's, now served as a pillow. He shook it loose with a little cry.

"Thanks, old man, I'll handle him," said Faith.

Rodney's eyes roamed wildly. "She's gone to powder her nose," said Stone and pulled his bulk to the table. "See here," said Stone, "you write stuff about horses—do you know anything about dogs?"

Rodney shook his head; he could not speak.

"Because," Stone said, "if you don't, I'll tell you something. That setter over there with that old sot is a fine animal. It's got fine points—or don't you believe me?"

Suddenly Rodney was alone—the little lovely one had deserted him; Faith's shoulder, supporting Slope, was disappearing past the bar; even his hostess had gone into communion with the zombi—he was dreadfully, ineluctibly alone in a crucible of smoke and tomtoms and angry interrogations out of the red mouth of Sirius.

"You can't fool me on dogs," challenged Stone and Rodney shuddered.

"Oh no," he moaned, "oh no, I wouldn't!"

"Mad," insisted Mrs Danby; "he's right—we're mad. This is only my second collins but I should like to do a rhumba. Do you think that rather odd?"

But Trimble did not answer. He had lifted his head, and Mrs Danby, trailing his expression across the taproom, saw two people who interested her because they plainly interested Trimble.

CHAPTER SEVEN
PAST TWILIGHT

J OE heard the car, heard the brake screek and the motor die
in a last cough. That might be Carl Schaeffer, but if it was,
he couldn't help it now; he must do what Mrs Gillibo asked. He
waited until the silence—the country silence haunted by insect
sounds and a dog howling far off and a moth thumping at a
screen close by—made him conscious of himself, and his confes-
sion, and her, and the store like a coop confining them. He took
his cigar from his mouth and said, "You ready to go?"

Selena was looking beyond him, past the snug cans and
boxes of an interior as familiar to her as the inside of her shoe,
to the point where the light stopped. It stopped abruptly, bril-
liantly, on the copper mesh of the screen, no more able to escape
than the moth to get in, for the country dark had come suddenly
into Little Salem, over its street, onto its porches, shutting bright
doors and windows though they stood wide open. Selena, intent,
might have been guessing what the night concealed.

She knew. That rattle and screek, that final cough, were
unmistakable. In a minute he might come in the door or he might
go around to the back and enter through the curtain, but that she
must face Emil seemed as certain as that the car had brought no
other. And she did not want to face him. All anger stood behind
her with the brooding and the wishing; she had made her decision and, helped by chance, in her mind had as good as carried it
out. Her chest swelled.

"Look," she said, and Joe's eyes shifted with her pointing finger, "that's my bag. You take it out to your car and I'll be right with you. Okay?"

"Sure." He picked up the heavy suitcase and she watched him go with a throb of satisfaction at the quickness and ease with which the thing was done. Her purse lay on the counter. She opened it, took out a pair of gloves, noticed Joe's change, dropped it with the other silver and closed the purse. She tucked it under one arm and shook out the gloves.

Several minutes later, when a motor started, followed by a curving flash across the dark, she still stood there, fiddling at the white knitted gloves.

Joe, holding back the screen, said, "Ready?"

Selena pushed the gloves into her purse and with firm, quick steps went out the store.

For a while, after this, silence descended. The electric bulb burned nakedly. Insects beat at it. Far off a dog howled. A moth thumped the screen. Beyond the curtain Grandfather Gillibo woke. "S'lena?" he called. "Selena?"

The curtain stirred and Emil Gillibo noiselessly entered.

2

Night always changed the road, though you knew it as well as you knew your own lane. When you were driving and there was no moon, night rubbed out the land and left you only what was in the beam's throw and this, rushing at you so fast and so separated from the dark, was first mysterious and then surprising in its sudden familiarity and you drove with a kind of exultation as of a conqueror who makes the unknown known. Your father would say slow, Son, slow, if there wasn't another beam in sight for a mile ahead or a mile behind and this got you so irritated that you hated the night and hated the road and couldn't get home quick enough. You drove faster and that made him worse and that made you worse and the driving became a chore and the vanished exultation something else he had spoiled. But Selena, as you drove, said nothing. It was swell. You would have liked to drive a long way.

You found yourself wondering why, back there in the store, you thought of her as Mrs Gillibo and why, now in the car, you began to think of her as Selena. That was what nearly everybody called her, but you never had. You seldom called anybody by first names—it was Mr Faith and Mr Buckmeister and Mr Trimble— unless it was somebody that didn't amount to much, like Emil Gillibo, or somebody you grew up with, like Eunice Littleton, or somebody you just liked, like Holland Heinschmidt. Selena was different. She amounted to something and you hadn't grown up with her; she was grown when you were a kid, and you never knew her well enough to like her; you were just shy of her. But back there in the store, when you opened up, you had forgotten all that and talked to her as you might have talked to Holland. Maybe you did like her all the time, and when she asked you to do something for her you jumped at it because you liked her and were grateful to her for listening. And now, when you did her a favor, things were evened up and she wasn't Mrs Gillibo any more; she was Selena.

But the whole business was a funny thing just the same. Generally you hated and despised talking about yourself. That fellow Trimble, always asking fool questions—imagine opening up to him! Or anybody else, for that matter, including your own father and mother. Why, here, lately, you'd got so you almost always lied to Ma. I'll be back soon, you said; I got to run a fellow over to Madison, you said, and you didn't give her time to ask what fellow, knowing she wanted only another word to get anxious. That was the trouble with Ma, she got anxious whatever you said, so it was better to say nothing or else make up a tale. You might open up to Mr Faith, but Mr Faith generally guessed it before you said it; you never got a chance to open up. Like you did in the store to Mrs Gillibo—to Selena.

A funny thing. When you were talking to her you felt that you could tell her anything, not alone how you felt about the Harvest Home and all those people but a lot of other things—Little Salem and the farm and your father and maybe going out West somewhere. If it had been Emil in the store, you never would have opened up, or if it had been anybody else, even Carl Schaeffer, you would have kept your trap shut. It was a funny thing how you knew it was okay to talk to her and it was a funny thing still, knowing still that it was okay.

The pale diagonal of 28 bisected the beam and Joe slowed for the turn.

"Listen," he said, "this is how I feel, Selena——"

So that was what was eating him. It wasn't just those old hens at the Harvest Home; it was Little Salem and the farm and all the rest of it. Fed up with his old man. Fed up with slaving for the other fellow. Fed up with not getting anywhere and maybe losing what little he had. Fed up and at the same time hungry—for someplace, for something else.

She nodded, a motion faint in the instrument board's glow. "I know, I've felt that way a many a time myself. You know what, Joe"—she could laugh at it now, having left it behind—"you know what I spent half the afternoon doing? Wishing I was in New York—at a show—or a nightclub—or just wandering around—or maybe in a beauty parlor under one of those machines they got!"

"Yeah," he said, "New York. Yeah."

He drove steadily, not seeing her, not seeing the night, only the road. Machines. They were fabulous, like tales in a book—burnished, intricate, beautiful in their precision and their power, yet practical as a hayrake, and yours if you but had the money.

"I saw a movie once," she said, and as she described it—the miracle of the permanent, the rinse, the mudpack, the massage—he thought of movies he had seen and in the beam's path saw again the tall grain fall and, like the guns of surrendered armies, clustered in stacks before the invincible march of the machines.

"Listen, Selena—lemme tell you about a movie I saw. ... "

And she let him tell, indifferent to what was in the telling except that it brought a pulse to his eyes and drove his hand in excitement from the wheel. He was a funny boy; you'd think, the way he talked, it was more farm he wanted instead of an end to farming. But she smiled and nodded, contemplating in the dark windshield her transformed self as in a mirror.

"I know, Joe. Sometimes, alone in the store—or I might as well be alone for anybody I got to talk to—I get so crazy!"

"Wanting to talk to somebody? Je's, I could die——"

"Yeah, so could I. Like tonight—I thought if I could just go somewhere——"

"Me too. It's swell riding, ain't it?"

3

At one end of the long littered table, with both hands holding a pile of unwashed dishes, Mrs Purdy let her burden rest for a breath on the table's edge, let her eyes flit down the board. It had the higgledy-piggledy appearance of the aftermath of a storm or a battle. Had some great horn of plenty burst and beasts rooted in the debris, the effect would have been similar. Here a half-chewed sandwich nuzzled half-gnawed chicken bones; there hacks of butter swam ruinously in gravy. All that good food, mourned Mrs Purdy through her spectacles—to be thrown out when it should be swimming in men's gastric juices.

The thought lingered but lightly in the upper creases of her cerebrum, for Mrs Purdy at this moment could be compared to the business executive who sits with three telephones before him and a secretary at each elbow; under her passing recognition of the state of the table layers and layers of other thoughts demanded Mrs Purdy's attention, though in her case no system waited to serve her.

Presently she was confronted not only with reducing this clutter to order but with ordering the lives of the humans that made it. The husbands, having eaten, must digest comfortably. The children must behave yet be happy. The wives, though assisting her, must by her be assisted. And these responsibilities, involving such a varied number of persons, involved more than immediate action; they involved action in the future, for which the Harvest Home was Mrs Purdy's opportunity, in the language of business, to "contact" folk. Mrs Purdy was not a busybody or a martinet; she was a neighbor and a friend. Thus her thoughts, crowding upward and upward, informed her that the Reeser twins needed a bath if ever young ones did; that if Mr Ben Davis didn't write his check for the Ladies' Aid tonight, she might not catch him for a month; that something ought to be done about that crack in the ceiling; that old Mrs Fisher had looked neglected and pouty; she must surely seek her out and soothe her; that the Sunday-school room badly wanted painting and it was up to her to bully the deacons before Ella Mastick bullied them for new hymnbooks; that Lance, unless she guarded him, would talk politics too soon after supper; that this was Friday and tomorrow Saturday, and that, if she didn't make haste, those women in the kitchen were careless enough to chip Mrs Henry Norton's luster pitcher which Freddy, when he brought the lemonade (And where on earth was the child?), said Grandma particularly asked her to wash personally and separate. Under these and a multitude of matters relating to others Mrs Purdy's interbrain held in suspense a whole mass of data relating to herself—her home, her flowers, her livestock, her larder; her baking, canning, sewing, laundering; her daily routine from sunup to prayer and her problems that were a part yet outside of it, from chickens unexpectedly sick to the snowball bush she was going to prune if ever she had the time. Among the mass was an injunction about cobwebs. "I must sweep those cobwebs in the parlor." For thirty years Mrs Purdy had been reminding her hands to sweep cobwebs and for thirty years, regularly, her hands had been obeying. The cobwebs always came back. Someday they would come back when there would be no hands to dust, no watchman to warn; the cobwebs would win. But whenever such a terror shook Mrs Purdy she resolutely erased it and where it had leered she resolutely stamped: sweep cobwebs! And below the cobwebs and the snowball and all the other usual and extra impedimenta of her day, pushing at them like sprouts while they in turn pushed at the roots overlaying them, Mrs Purdy did not utterly bury her social imperatives. They included, though she herself did not so classify them, a number of funerals scheduled or impending, besides weddings, anniversaries, church events and various visitations, for "company," whether she entertained company or was company, was as vital as religion in her life. No week passed that the Madison *Gazette* did not name her in the Little Salem social news; no instant when, consciously or subconsciously, she was not scheming gayety in her fashion. Will we ever make that drive to Atlantic City? Maybe next holiday, maybe the holiday after. Up the question pushed, past the sick chickens, past the slippery deacons, as it had this summer and many summers long—pushed up, saluted wistfully and stood by. And deeper yet, never quite forgotten, never relinquished, waiting, too, their not impossible hour, droused in their secret fissures a pheasant's feather, a scrap of red brocade that would make a lovely dress, yellow clippings of verses she once had fancied and with the printed verses lines written in faded ink, *Ode to Autumn,* by Helen Hollins Purdy ....

Mrs Purdy thrust the dishes to firmer support on the table and with them seemed to deposit the cabinet of her mind. She asked the Lord and those women in the kitchen to forgive her. She wished she wasn't such a muggins, but, after all, desertion would take but a few minutes.

"Eunice dear," she said to Eunice Littleton, who had come into the room, "will you tell Ella Mastick I'll be right back? And please to leave Mrs Norton's luster pitcher? I won't be a shake!"

"Of course, Mrs Purdy——"

"Thank you, Eunice."

Such a dear girl, such a pretty girl. She'd often thought that if Joe had to get interested in some girl—but there, Joe didn't look at them, didn't look at any of them, and in a way that was why she fretted—if he was here now with the other young folks, playing games like she used to play when she was young—instead of traipsing off so sudden-like with that dark, tight scowl on his face he'd worn all through supper—why, she wouldn't fret a bit if he'd smiled and patted her shoulder and said, "Ma, it's all right——"

She crossed the church porch and, panting a little because she had hurried, descended a step. The darkness, rushing over her that way, blinded her and she could see nothing, hear nothing but the distant howling of a dog. Then she perceived that their car was not where they had parked it. Her eyes caught the flicker of a taillight near the railroad tracks and her ears the faint jolt of tires.

Mrs Purdy stood looking after the lost light with a queer feeling such as she had not met in years. She recognized it as helplessness. She was surprised, too, to find her spectacles fogged.

It's perspiration, she told herself—it's a very hot night. You're a muggins, Helen Purdy, said Mrs Purdy to Mrs Purdy, and she took off her spectacles and wiped them on her apron and went back inside the church and rescued those dishes from Eunice Littleton, who had paused to nibble an olive.

4

A dog howled somewhere, three midges died suddenly on the light, and Emil moved with loose, whispering strides. There was none of the lag, as if infirmity or a fear hobbled him, of his characteristic gait; unobserved, he seemed to step out like a man clear of snake-grass. His shoes made no sound; his corduroys, rubbing, whispered.

He stooped at the counter, opening the cash drawer. When he closed it the contortion of his face was not disappointment or anger but a fatalistic grin. He stood straight and looked all around the store, starting with the shelves nearest him and going from shelf to shelf, up, down, around, around, until his shifting eyes completed the circle. Whatever this survey showed or failed to show him he appeared not dissatisfied nor yet convinced, for he began a closer inspection, taking down goods and peering behind them and, here and there, shaking containers and opening several.

Whatever he sought he kept nothing, and if his quest was money he was oddly indifferent to the discovery, on a high shelf, of a small jar stuffed with coins. He dumped these into his palm, sneered and spat to the floor from the ladder he had mounted. He returned the coins to the jar and the jar to its perch and climbed down with another saturnine grin. But when he had removed the ladder he came back and with the sole of a foot carefully rubbed out the spittle. Once more, with finality, he surveyed the shelves before he abandoned them.

This search, which took a while, proceeded amid a pandemonium to which Emil paid less heed than if he had been separated from it by mountains instead of three yards of cambric. Grandfather Gillibo had given up his petulant cries to solace himself with the radio. When Emil turned on a lamp the old man raised his head, straining directly into the glare.

"S'lena?"

Emil clicked the light and clicked it again, off, on. He watched his grandfather who sat as still and unwinking as a frog in a bull's-eye's ray. After a moment, muttering, the old man lowered his head. The Hawaiian guitars whanged on. Emil, his corduroys whispering, ransacked the room.

He had circled it and was rubbing his hands before the dark doorway to the kitchen when Grandfather Gillibo raised his head again. A dial of the radio snapped. The music ceased. Emil, rubbing his hands, watched the strained face in the lamplight.

"Get out of here!" shouted Grandfather Gillibo suddenly. "You, Emil—get out of here!"

Emil grinned, took three steps, kicked the radio's plug out of its socket and went into the kitchen.

Here, for some twenty minutes, he examined the cupboards and their contents minutely while, in the room he had left, his grandfather cursed him between intermittent sobs to which Emil seemed oblivious except for the occasional shadow of his grin. When at last he had replaced each object as it was he lit an oil lantern and quit the kitchen by a short flight of steps descending into the yard.

Insects beat at the lantern and, where he set it down, made a smudge around it. There was a pile of refuse here in a corner of the fence. Emil rummaged, kicking through mash and rinds until he had isolated all the empty cans and bottles. He sniffed them one by one, and a small vial which he sniffed several times he did not throw back with the others but snubbed under a heap of lumber. When he stood up the sag of his chin in the lantern's glow was peculiarly sharp and exhausted. He looked dead beat. He looked like a fox run long before the dogs. The bell in the store jangled and Emil picked up the lantern and retraversed the yard.

Mr and Mrs Lance Purdy waited in the store.

"How are you, Emil?" Mrs Purdy said, adding in the same breath, "And Mrs Gillibo—and your grandfather—all well?"

Emil said they were all well and Mrs Purdy put down the basket she was carrying and remarked on Mr Gillibo's wonderful constitution. It reminded her, she said, of the constitution of her niece-by-marriage's great-grandfather who was still living near Ringoes at the age of a hundred and four. Now there was really a wonderful constitution....

Emil did not stir from his drawn position near the curtain, his head half averted in that way he had. Lance Purdy paced nervously back and forth and picked his teeth. Mrs Purdy talked on. When the cursing began she turned pink but she did not stop.

"Excuse me," Emil said to the Purdys.

He gripped Grandfather Gillibo's shoulder hard as he bent above him. "Stop it, you old fool—stop it—company's here—Mrs Purdy's here." Grandfather Gillibo gasped and whimpered a little. Emil bore down on his shoulder and Grandfather Gillibo cried out once. "Here," said Emil and put the plug in the socket. Professor Pundit's Question Bee flooded them, drowning Grandfather Gillibo's sob in its hearty humor.

"You mean son of a bitch," sobbed Grandfather Gillibo.

In the store Mrs Purdy shook her head. "Poor man," she said vaguely, "such a trial. Emil," she said, "if your grandfather suffers bad from his sciatica, I heard about a new remedy——"

"Look here, Gillibo," interrupted Lance Purdy, "that boy of mine——"

"Now, Lance, you mustn't excite yourself. Emil ain't interested——"

"—went off in our car more 'n an hour ago. We been——"

"He had to drive a fellow over to Madison," said Mrs Purdy, blinking rapidly, smiling her hardest. "Maybe he broke down or maybe he got delayed someway. Lance is worried about him, though I tell him there's no need to fret, Joe's all right. Meantime we waited and everybody's gone——"

Emil relaxed.

"I'll run you home," he stated flatly.

He limped out of the store and Mrs Purdy, before they followed him, looked reproachfully at Lance Purdy. "Ain't you ashamed," she said, "belittling Joe to a fellow like that?"

Purdy was silent while she talked the mile away. Only once did Emil speak, when she was telling about the rats. "Like I say, Joe shoots them after we catch them in the traps. I'm too tender-hearted to watch, but Joe says sometimes——"

"Do you ever use poison?" Emil said.

"Law, no! It's too expensive and I'd be afraid for the chickens."

They were at Purdys' gate then and Emil said he wouldn't come in; he had to get back to the store. But he lingered a moment.

"We got a lot of rats," he said. "Maybe sometime you'll lend me Joe's gun, huh?"

"Why, sure," said Mrs Purdy. "Any time, Emil—any time. Now if you like."

Grandfather Gillibo, in the empty house, twisted the dead dials. He did not know that a tube had burned out. He sucked his plate and cried.

CHAPTER EIGHT
THE TAPROOM

I wish I could believe you," said John Faith to Trimble's statement. "I wish I could believe, if that's what you mean, that a man may control his destiny even as far as from here to the can—or as long as it took Harve to pass out. I hope you don't mind my referring to the can, ma'am."

"Not at all," said Mrs Danby. "Whatever else would one call it?"

"All right," said John Faith to Trimble. "You bought a farmhouse and you made it over to your heart's desire and you'll live in it and love it the rest of the summer and maybe the rest of your days and all this comes to pass because you so will it—you think. But what about Bermuda? What about the Duncans? What about me happening by that particular week end? And what about whatever it was about that particular place that caused you to put a binder on it that particular day when a day later another party might have beat you to it? It was chance, chance—all along the line."

Trimble, remembering a marble haply scuffed in passing, tried to laugh and repressed a small shiver instead. "You're hopeless, John."

"But time and chance happeneth to them all," quoted Rodney gloomily.

"Exactly," nodded Faith. "To them all. I wish it didn't, but it does. So three friends of Harve's start out yesterday to plan their future and so they wind up tonight in a hospital lucky to have a future left, let alone a plan for it. And alongside of them lies the driver of a milk truck who doubtless planned, until they hit him, to spend his Fourth of July on a picnic in the Poconos with a girl who will now marry a merry-go-round proprietor she never saw till today. The same chance not only knocks your own life cockeyed but maybe half a dozen others. 'I won't take chances,' you say and chance rides out of nowhere on a crazy Cadillac and takes you."

"Oh, come now," said Trimble, "I'm not arguing free will can rule forces like sudden death. I only said——"

"From battle and murder and from sudden death, good Lord, deliver us," intoned Rodney.

"And neither am I harping on disaster," Faith declared. "I suppose chance is responsible for as much joy as it is misery. For example, let's look at your pretty niece, ma'am——"

They all looked at her, where the rest of the baseball team, gaping at such a conquest under a right fielder's chin, quite evidently envied a palooka who couldn't hit .150 in any other league, and Stone looked with umbrage and Rodney with considerable doubt as to whether he saw a niece at all.

"No, John," said Mrs Danby, "your point's no good. You don't know Bibby. That wasn't chance."

"But wasn't it?" About to go on, Faith checked himself and she wished he wouldn't look at her so frankly humbly and yet was glad he did. "Don't worry," he said quietly. "Perry Titcomb's all right. His father owns half of Dooley Township and Perry goes to Yale."

She was annoyed at him for his calm implication and annoyed at herself for not asserting with some heat that her grandfather had toted a hod and she didn't care if Beatrice picked up a coal miner and why on earth did John Faith treat her, at the oddest moments, as if she were the lady of the manor. She stopped because conscience reminded her that she probably was a snob. Witness: she had simply nothing in the world against Mr Stone, the poor stinker, except that he wasn't a gentleman. But how hellish to be always so aware, particularly of one's own integrity.

"See here," said Stone and she felt his chivalry rising and deplored it, "I'll go over and bounce that fellow if you say the word."

Mrs Danby said, "Please—no——"

John Faith said, "Better leave the bouncing to Gunderson; it's his job."

Rodney, who apparently had been listening to nobody, burst into high laughter.

"What's funny?" Stone demanded.

"What's funny? My dear man, everything's funny; the whole world is funny; it is the most excrutiatingly, uproariously humorous glob of dust and gas—it's—it's a belly laugh—by the comic in a celestial burlesque show—and we sit here—inside the burp!—jabbering of free will and joy and whatnot—while flatulence creates another Eden and the gods roar!"

Rodney roared with the gods, the tears running down his cheeks. His companions studied whatever else they could.

"I don't think that's funny," Stone said, "and," truculently, "I don't think it's nice talk."

"Oh dear," said Mrs Danby, "we all seem to be so quarrelsome. Can't we agree on something?"

"Say, Stone"—Faith captured Stone's attention and Rodney's shaking shoulder with the same gesture—"I heard you talking about dogs. Maybe you can give me some advice. Was a fellow over by Frenchtown had a pointer bitch. ... "

In the lee of the discussion Trimble welcomed Mrs Danby's sigh and the pressure of her returning arm.

"There's no convincing John, is there?" he said.

"I think he's a dear," said Mrs Danby.

"Yes—but an awful faker. To hear him talk, you'd say he was a complete defeatist, with no more incentive to live than a blind man has to get up for the sunrise. Yet he works his thumbs off, mostly, it's true, for other people. Half the stuff he talks is pop-pycock. He's actually a sentimentalist and believes in miracles. I ought to know—he's been most extraordinarily kind to me."

"I still think he's a dear," Mrs Danby said.

Trimble, disconcerted, employed the corner of his eye and decided, by her absent manner, that she hadn't meant to be rude; she merely wasn't listening. The experience was not new and he sighed, the familiar taste of ineffectuality bitter on his tongue.

He said abruptly, "There's someone I want to speak to. Do you mind?"

Mrs Danby gave him her full attention with her smile. "Of course I don't. But you'll come right back, won't you?"

Trimble said he would.

Joe Purdy saw him rise and watched him, as Trimble squeezed past a table and stepped aside for Beatrice and Perry Titcomb to execute a dance step, with foreboding. That fellow had to come nosing around with his handshakes and his questions no matter where you were. You'd think once in a day was enough to shake hands with a fellow.

"A guy's coming," he said, "Trimble, that owns Heinschmidts' place."

Selena made no comment. She had spoken but a few words since they sat down and he had said less, the spell that fused them in the car broken from the moment they entered Valley Inn. He had drawn up as she directed at Valley Service, which was the stop for all the busses, and he had gotten out and helped her alight and put her bag on the stoop outside the office with the excitement of talk still tingling him and no room for other reflections save regret that the ride was over. For the first time he had asked her where she was going.

He had not thought then there was anything curious about her answer. "New York," she had said and added, as a person might who admits anything can happen, "I guess."

"But look here," he had argued, "the New York bus won't be through for an hour yet. You don't want to just wait, do you?"

"No," she had said, "I don't specially want to wait."

She was standing faced away from him, away from the bus office toward the highway and the headlights of cars approaching from both directions, slowing at the traffic signal and going on. In this illuminated spot, directly under the flare of the gasoline pumps, he saw her clearly as he had in the store, the dark neat hair, the level brows, the mouth that had surprised him by smiling—everything that made her Mrs Gillibo. But now, either their conversation of the last half hour or a haphazard realization that he was taller than she or something unlike Mrs Gillibo in her present attitude, her weight on one foot, a droop to the near shoulder, changed her from the storewife into someone who bothered him a lot.

"Well, you ain't figuring on hitchhiking, are you?" he had joked to cover this uprush of disquiet that was almost pity.

She had answered, the same brooding in her voice that was in her eyes on the passing cars, "You would think it was pretty terrible if I did, wouldn't you?"

That had floored him; that was a sticker, you know; that left a fellow not sure where he was or hardly what she meant, and so he had mumbled, "Gosh, no—pretty terrible?—of course I wouldn't—but hitchhiking—gosh—you wouldn't do that—gee, if you gotta get to New York tonight——"

With that she had turned her eyes and the smile was in them. She had cocked her head like a hen bird at a sudden sound and she had said with calm decisiveness, "I wouldn't let you drive me to New York, Joe. But you can keep me company for a little bit—you can buy me a drink or something—and maybe we'll talk some more, huh?"

Why, sure, he had said; why, sure he would, and he had put the bag back into the car and swung across the highway to the Inn, and they were out and going up the steps, the taproom's chilled air blowing his face and Selena's sleeve brushing him where he held the door open; they had crossed the border of sheltering darkness and wavering light and vagrant sound into Crazyville—for so the taproom struck him as foreign, raucous, menacing, alluring—they were settled at the table and had ordered their beers before his excitement's haze cleared to familiar faces—Perry Titcomb's, Al Mayhew's, Mr Faith's—and he began to think of his mother and father and the Harvest Home. He had shut his mind almost roughly. Somebody would take them home. The hell with that.

Doc McKasker saw them come in and revolved his body at the bar. He said, with his back to Mayhew, "Now ain't that funny—speak of the devil——"

His smile gloated like a magician's after the rope trick. "Maybe it ain't funny to you. Maybe you didn't guess who I meant awhile ago. And maybe that's just as well. I still can't figure it out," said Doc McKasker, almost to himself. "I never saw a fellow in such a sweat and not letting on what he was in a sweat about. 'Are you sure?' he says. 'Are you sure you didn't sell her anything lately or fill a prescription for her? Any poison?' he said. That made me a little mad, you know, and I says to him, 'Well, now, look here, Mr So and So, and supposing I did, and supposing I sold you something that maybe you didn't want your wife to know about, and supposing she came in here snooping around to ask me what it was, do you think I'd let on; do you think I'd tell her your business and my business?" And with that he gave me the funniest look like I'd hit him where he lived and out he hops without a good-by or a so long or nothing else—and good riddance to him!

"I tell you, Allie," said Doc McKasker, revolving, "I tell you something." He stopped, for Mayhew was not there. In the lobby Mayhew occupied the telephone booth; the door was shut tight; the receiver was at Mayhew's ear; his lips opened and closed, yet Mayhew did not seem to be talking. Doc McKasker rapped the bar. "Gimme another beer, Bill," he said aggrievedly.

Gunderson recognized the tone and foretold to the minute—
it would be two beers hence—when Doc McKasker would get his
feelings hurt. He wouldn't get them hurt about anything or by
anybody in particular; he would just get them hurt. Tears would
come into his eyes and he would start away, leaving his last beer
all but untouched. Gunderson would call him back and say, "You
owe for six beers, Doc," and Doc McKasker would pay for them,
including the last beer, which he would then finish with the look
of a victim at a holdup man, and whatever or whoever had hurt
his feelings before, it would be Gunderson who had hurt them
when he finally departed.

So the bartender took it on the chin coming or going—what
a life! Gunderson didn't know but he hated it worse than that
rubber's job in New York. You got 'em then with hangovers
instead of staggers and they were pretty sour, but at least you
could pound their bellies, the bastards. Guys like that Stone, so
stuck on their muscles they would lie in the hotroom admiring
their own legs with as much pleasure as if they were Dietrich's,
or guys like that old bird with Mrs Danby, no good any more
but kidding themselves that a firehose would shock them into
competition with Clark Gable. It was bastards like that he had
quit New York to get away from.

"Have you got any mints, Bill?" said Allison Mayhew.
Gunderson tossed out a pack of Breathems and refilled three
beers.

And here they were, the sour and greedy rich, all over the
place, crowding the highways, crowding the bars, buying the best
farms, posting the prettiest land, grabbing the country for themselves like they had grabbed all the dough and all the good jobs in
town. But at that, they weren't any worse than the people already
here. Not any worse than a hick ball team trying to be a bunch
of Yales, or a drugstore doc acting like a Park Avenue special-
ist, or the president of the Community Club anxiously chewing
Breathems. If these country bastards were so stuck on city styles

and parties and giving those punk hayloft shows, why didn't they move to town and make room for somebody that really wanted the country? But oh no, unless you were born amongst 'em, they wouldn't even let you play cityfolks in the same yard. City or country, all alike, all bastards, voted Gunderson.

"Bis!" shouted Felixio. He got up; he poked out his pot like a cheer leader's baton; he applauded above it until everybody applauded. "Bis! bis! bis!" Beatrice and her partner bowed and waved; her smile on Felixio rivaled Mona Lisa's and Mae West's. Felixio barked a final bis and sat down hastily. "Watch those dog," he advised Havla. The rumble under a chair died in a yelp.

Shameless satisfaction expanded in Gunderson. He recognized that the boss was on the spot: either he stopped the jitterbugs and risked displeasing important customers or he encouraged them and got arrested for running a dance hall without a license. But even the nickelodeon seemed to work for that wop; in his dilemma it gave him a male quartet.

"Oh, come with me, my Phyllis dear, to yon blue mountain free," yearned the quartet. Gunderson listened with the bar towel icy in his grip. That was how it was once; that was how it was going to be—blue mountain and him and Sigrid—"where the blossoms smell the sweetest, oh, come along with me"—the blossoms pink and white on the apple trees, a red barn under the blue mountain and behind the trim little house a path through the fields to woods and a spring deeply cool and quiet, like the bar was sometimes in the long hot afternoons when Felixio slept and nobody came in.

"We'll have a cabin, Phyllis, a horse and pig and cow,
And you will mind the baby while I mind the——"

Gunderson slapped the towel at nothing. He rubbed the beery fixtures and brusquely commanded Sigrid to wait on that guy who had come in with John Faith and who was beckoning now from another table. The woman with him Gunderson had

seen before. The young fellow was a farmer by the look of him—
the lucky crumb—oh hell—and nuts to all male quartets.

"But you must let me buy you a drink," Trimble was insisting
after Joe had asked him if he knew Mrs Gillibo and Trimble had
bowed and said, of course, we're neighbors, aren't we? They both
sat down and Trimble said again, his pale eyes on Joe, "Neighbors.
In fact I felt very much the stranger till you two came in. It was
like—well, seeing someone from home. You know?"

It was like that, Joe Purdy, and it is like that still, my lad—
you in your store-bought clothes so utterly unsports; you in your
frayed shirt and washed ruddiness, you humble us—your smile
makes a celebrity's obscene; your clear eyes mortify a silly girl's
ogles—it is good, Joe, to see you and to remember here, in bedlam,
the earth and sky and sunny orchards—perhaps, Joe, through a
barroom's haze, there shall embrace spirits that groped blindly
on the Barrens.

"I'll have another beer," said Selena.

"Two beers and a scotch and soda," Trimble ordered.

A beer for Mrs Gillibo—a beer for my neighbor, that strange
woman who impales her customers on flypaper. When I look at
you, Mrs Gillibo, you are steel and smoke, mystery and mockery;
you are, indeed, the strange woman. Yet, strange woman with a
lad, you are also merely somebody in a cheap dress and a dowdy
hat. So I shall talk to you; I shall chat, and my conversation, Mrs
Gillibo, shall benignly and wittily smother you.

Trimble talked.

"Hi, Perry," said Joe Purdy to that girl's silky back between
them and all at once got over the fear that somebody would walk
over and say, outside, buddy, you don't belong here. He began to
feel all right; he began to look around. Valley Inn. He had passed
it a million times, he guessed, but whenever he wanted a beer and
figured his mother wouldn't smell it on him he went to Mike's
Bar-B-Q or the Cedars or some common place. City people went
to Valley Inn, week-end people, horse people, field-trials people;

people like the bunch with John Faith. Yet a place that would stand for old man Havla, who couldn't get in Mike's with his dogs any more, must not be such hot stuff. A funny thing how he began to feel all right as soon as that fellow butted in. That fellow was a pain in the ass, but somehow when he came around another fellow could take comfort. Maybe it was because he did all the talking and you didn't have to talk; you didn't even have to listen. Trimble was talking now about a trip he had made somewhere. The names, Curacao, La Guaira, Caracas, stirred him like the singing. Joe leaned back, politely smiling, and thought about Holland Heinschmidt and South America and Flash Gordon and what Mr Faith had said about the sun in your sap at the end of the day.

Mrs Danby decided that she had better break it up. "Your nice friend has abandoned me for another woman and I wish," she wheedled, "you'd come out of the kennels. Men are so delighted when they can speak of bitches; I positively resent it," she confessed.

John Faith dropped Stone in the middle of belligerent rebuttal.

"Madam——"

"Please—I don't like that word either—there's something or other about it——"

"I'm sorry. Lady——"

"No!"

"Ma'am?"

Mrs Danby's eyes chastised him behind their laughter and behind their laughter they were wistful.

"The name is Gretchen—I don't know why, but it is—it's not difficult to pronounce—G-r-e-t-c-h-e-n, Gretchen—a number of people can say it—and I've even revealed it publicly on deeds and titles. You know? Those things real-estate men look up in the county clerk's office?"

Stone choked a snort. Those two—mooning at each other while the best of his argument died in his throat. She had deliberately interrupted. It was outrageous—one of these women who thought she was Mrs Astor. If he wasn't a gentleman he would tell her she had damn bad manners.

"Listen," said John Faith—for a moment his hand touched hers, but his eyes escaped and roved—"did I ever tell you about Harve Slope and the baby chicks?"

Oh, man, man, why do you run away from me?

"This fellow Slope is an incurable romantic. He's not a rounder; he just believes in romance—he really believes in it— but he'll fall in love with any girl that smiles on him. And the trouble is Harve never stops to think whether she likes the idea or not, whether she's married, single or in love with another guy; he's a simplehearted fellow and he goes for romance in a simplehearted way. And another thing—Harve, as you may have noticed, drinks. It makes him contrary and impetuous. Well, there was this woman; she wasn't a bad sort of woman but she was an unhappy woman, and when Harve looked at her she looked right back at him—I suppose because there was nobody else in sight at the moment. This woman was living then—never mind where, it was a long time ago; it was when Harve first came out here; it was before you came out here—in nineteen and thirty-three, wasn't it?"

"Yes," said Mrs Danby. He remembers the year. But why is he telling me this? Is he just running, running away?

"I say——" tried Stone vainly.

"In nineteen and thirty-three. Yes, it was before that. This woman's husband—who clerked at the hotel where they were living—he wasn't a happy man either. He was jealous and I suppose there were other reasons. But Harve didn't care anything about that. Harve took to haunting the hotel bar and he took to giving her presents, crazy things like an archery set and mail-order hats and things only Harve could think of, and the woman put up with him and put up with the presents, though she couldn't have thought much of either. Her husband always found out about the presents and he forced or stole them from her—he was a weak sort of man—and he always broke them or tore them up where Harve would run onto them. He never said a word to Harve but he hated Harve, and I guess he hated his wife, too, in his weak, queer way. He was scared of her—once he asked me a queer thing, whether you could taste poison in coffee—but we'll skip that; it has nothing to do with this story. To cut it short, one night when Harve was in the bar she said something that gave him an inspiration. I never knew exactly what she said, only what Harve believed she said. He called me up at home—he was pretty drunk but he could still talk and he was very excited—he called me up and asked me where he could buy a hundred baby chicks. Well, after all, you don't go out shopping for baby chicks in the middle of the night."

"Jugtown—best poultry in the state on a certain farm near Jugtown," asserted Stone.

Faith nodded while Rodney, glassy eyed, frowned in haughty disapproval of them all.

"Maybe so. But I wasn't getting out of bed to hunt baby chicks near Jugtown or anywhere else and I told Harve that. 'But you've got to,' he said; 'Selena wants them.' The woman's name wasn't Selena; it was something like that. 'Why does she want a hundred baby chicks tonight?' I said. 'She doesn't,' Harve said; 'she just wants one chick, but by the great horn spoon'—that's what he said, the great horn spoon—'if she wants one chick, I'll give her a hundred!' Of course I told him he was drunk and to go to bed and get the chicks in the morning, but if you tell Harve he's drunk, that only makes him more bullheaded, so he hung up on me and he went out and got a hundred baby chicks by himself—I don't know where and I don't know how—and at four o'clock in the morning he showed up at the hotel with all those chicks cheeping and squawking and made such a racket unloading the crates that Selena, I mean the woman, came down and gave him the bawling out of his life. I guess she was finally fed up; I guess the last thing in the world she wanted was chicks. But Harve couldn't understand; it seemed to him she was mighty unappreciative and he was shocked and it sort of broke his heart. Harve is a tender kind of man under all that bluster. And what happened later in the morning didn't help any, even if it was the husband's doing and not hers—when Harve woke up around noon and found every one of those baby chicks on his front porch with their throats cut."

"How awful!" gasped Mrs Danby.

Stone wet his lips. "I don't believe that story," he said slowly.

"I assure you it happened." John Faith did not smile. "But that isn't all—it isn't even the point."

"Is the point any more bearable?" asked Mrs Danby.

"That depends on how you look at it. I didn't know at the time why Selena—that is, the woman—wanted a baby chick or rather how Harve got it into his head that she did. I didn't know for several years."

He paused and, though noise and music swirled around them, their attention, even Rodney's, did not waver.

"I got to know this woman a little; I got to talk to her and sometimes she would talk to me. As I said, she wasn't a bad sort of woman, common maybe and not much education, but life hadn't given her a hell of a lot and she wanted something more than to grow old in a little country town and finally just die. So one day we were talking, about the styles that year, about what women were wearing, and she spoke this word that suddenly gave me the clue to the whole business. Whatever it was we were talking about, whatever it was women were wearing, she said she liked it; she said she liked anything that was chick."

To Rodney's stare Faith said, after a moment, "She'd seen it in the women's magazines—she read them regularly."

"Chick?" echoed Rodney. "Chick!—chick!—chick!" His laughter roared.

Stone said, "I don't believe it. I don't believe one man would cut all those little chickens' throats."

Faith shrugged. He leaned back. He did not look at Mrs Danby.

She said, low, "That was a hateful story. Why did you tell it?"

Faith shrugged again.

"And it wasn't funny—I'm sorry for the woman."

"But so am I," Faith assured her.

Mrs Danby turned away. Trimble was approaching through the smoke. "Here comes our hermit," said Mrs Danby lightly. "The poor man doesn't look very happy."

At the table Trimble had left, Selena said, "He's a nance."

"Gosh—do you think so?"

"Anyway, I don't like him."

"Neither do I, S'lena."

"I'm sorry he was here. He gives me the willies."

"Me too! But that's funny—that's exactly what I was thinking when he came up. It's funny you thought so too."

Selena regarded him placidly. She smiled a little. "I guess you and me think alike about a lot of things."

"Yeah," said Joe. He ran a finger around his collar. "Yeah," he said.

Selena said, "Do you want another beer?"

"I dunno——"

"Because I've got that change you left on the counter. I picked it up. I meant to tell you."

"Why—sure—if you want another——"

Selena looked into her glass. It was half full.

"I don't know as I want another," she said.

In the booth Stone got up.

"I'm going to have a look at that dog," he said to John Faith.

"The setter?"

"Yes," said Stone. He wheeled away, slapping his boots with his crop.

CHAPTER NINE
THE BARRENS: NIGHT

THERE was no moon and many stars but made the night the blacker. The night had the quality of black plush, soft and yielding yet impenetrable. The stars glowed hot and very low save one red star that moved slowly from west to east and disappeared high in the plush while a drumming sound swelled and faded. This was a plane heading into Newark Airport. There was no wind. Even the locusts were still and fireflies winked as if they were suspended by threads against the breathless woods.

Where Havla's house crouched on the ridge of the watershed a tone thinner than the night prevailed. It was not so much the light from one window as reflection from whitewash and cleared ground. Here the plush seemed worn. A body might navigate it without a hand held out for guidance. Into this pallor from the shadow of the eaves Pearly Havla stepped.

She squatted briefly while her eyes pierced the dark and made out the barn and the nearer trees and fence posts along the lane. When she rose she finished gnawing the bone in her teeth and tossed it into a rosebush. She wiped her hands on her dress and licked her fingers. She listened, motionless as the bush.

From inside the house, whining on and on, came a fretful monochord like a trapped bee's. She could see the baby as she had left it, face and fists scrooged tight, button mouth round and drooly, and she wished again there had been sugar to make it a sugar-tit. She could see the twins, too, asleep on the cot, and Loretta and Calvin, who was the oldest next to her, sprawled on the mattress on the floor. She hoped none of them would wake up. She hoped the baby would stop crying soon. If the baby cried later, when she wasn't there, she couldn't help that.

The whine stopped suddenly. She listened a little longer to be sure. Down in the black a freight train labored, sending fat puffs across the Valley; a bird twittered as if it dreamed badly, and in the barn Charlie, the horse, stamped twice and chuffed his cheeks in weary fellowship with the freight. Pearly tiptoed to the fence, avoided the gate with its pin and chain and slid under barbed wire. She ran sure footed along the lane until she reached the bend. Now, if the baby cried, nobody could blame her any more than if she had been in China.

Ahead, the lane descended invisible between high banks and dense woods. She took it steadily but with slower steps, for though the lane was not strange to her and often traveled in the dead of winter when the ground was truly perilous, she had seldom ventured it so late, and this night, for all its softness and warm hush, concealed in its heart something secret that made her own heart beat fast. So she crossed two fingers of her right hand and every ten steps, solemnly counting them, repeated the charm in the hex book.

What it forfended, what thing was lurking in the woods, Pearly did not pretend to conjure. No gnomes and goblins threatened her who had never heard a fairy tale and whose fancy stopped at the borders of experience. The snake might rustle out of the woods, or a skunk or a fox or her father. But Pearly did not really fear these. She charmed against something intangible, the secret force in the night that could trick her while it was enticing her on. I'm going to find out; I'm going to find out. She sang silently her defiance and appeal to the night, though what it was—that ultimate great discovery beyond the small, beyond the words and reprimands and peeks, beyond the tug of her own sensories that for so long, it seemed, had haunted and confused and tantalized her—what it was would not matter very much, whether it pleased or harmed or disappointed, if the mystery itself were shattered; if to know at last replaced to wonder. I'm going to find out. Somewhere, somehow the night must tell her.

The lane leveled and the stars pushed back the trees. A line of fence posts, darker than the sky, marked the end of Havla's land. A sense of breadth came out of the air and in the blackness lights glimmered small and far away. The blackness seemed dropping from under Pearly's feet. She overlooked the Valley. There was the ripple of 28, there the fixed dots of roadhouses, there a clump of dots for a town and there and there isolated eyes of farms. Straight across blinked the beacon on Toy Mountain and the taillight of the freight climbing Copperhead Gap. The freight vanished altogether and a full minute afterward the last puff reached her.

Now she pulled up one stocking and more confidently went on, down through Purdys' fields and past their outbuildings and the house where an upper window shone. It was late for a Purdy not to be abed; she stuck out her tongue derisively. Then the path led her by the brook and up the hummock and she scrambled into the dirt road where a second lane branched off the opposite side. This was the lane to the old Heinschmidt farm and she skipped by its mouth quickly, for hereabouts she had said that she saw the snake and, for very indignation at the lie, the snake might be there. She had gone a hundred yards along the dirt road when the flash came out of Heinschmidts' lane and followed her. Pearly waited in her tracks and Laurence, swinging John Faith's car out of the ruts, never knew how close he shaved bigger trouble than manslaughter.

The sweat, however, was still rolling off him when her outcry was a mile behind. Boy, boy, did she cuss him it was better than did she be killed!

What Pearly called out was inarticulate even to herself, a shout of sheer impulse as the car veered and sped on. It was half hail and half insult and wholly startling in the effect it left, as if someone else had shouted and she was listening in the dust swirl for the shout to be repeated. The dark clapped down again and no voice came, only the smoothly retreating purr of the motor, and Pearly sucked in her breath to a tight, hurting limit. She let her breath go. What if the car hadn't stopped or even slowed? She had done something; she had yelled; the night had dared her and she had not "taken" the dare; she had flung the dare back and the next time she would shout again. Come on, night—I'm going to find out!

Seventy pounds of tinder in a cotton shift, she set her feet to the Little Salem road.

Grandfather Gillibo had struggled out of his chair and by himself, stabbing and shuffling, advanced until the curtain grazed his stick and then his face. He bunched the folds and hung onto them while the store communicated its emptiness to him. Through the screen Pearly watched him, motionless but ominous under the strong light.

She had come onto the porch impelled by the light and a pang of hunger. Now she fingered the three pennies in her pocket with indecision, for the old man had always awed her and she shrank from encountering him alone. But somebody besides him must be there and thought of the candy watered her mouth. She went in.

Did he see her; did he hear the bell? The old buzzard can hear plenty when he wants to, Emil used to say, joking her with a wink and a smirk. But Emil wasn't in sight; nobody was in sight but Grandfather Gillibo, bent a little in his door, clutching the curtain, leaning on his stick with his other hand.

Pearly hesitated. She didn't know what to do. Emil might be right, but saying hello to someone who couldn't hear gave her goose pimples to consider and to walk over and touch him was beyond her powers of rashness. She drew up one leg under her skirt. At that moment Grandfather Gillibo moved. But first something about him moved. His face craned into the light like an old anxious bird's and out of its eyeholes seeped bright, slow tears. She saw them reach his chin and his hand brush them in a convulsive stab that released his stick. As it clattered to the floor he stepped out, grasping, directly toward her.

Pearly screamed. She whirled, lost her balance and plunged into a bin of potatoes. She screamed again, tried to rise, slipped and would have fallen had not Emil, coming down the stairs, caught her. Her small, desperate body wrapped itself against him. Emil held her wrist fast.

"There!" said Emil. "I got you."

He leered across at his grandfather who had stopped, wavering, after one step.

"Wha'd you do to scare her?"

As if the futility of the question were its answer, he released Pearly and recovered the stick and put it in the old man's trembling hand.

"Go to bed!" he ordered. He propped his arms under the other's elbows.

Grandfather Gillibo resisted violently. "I want my raddio," he blubbered.

"He wants his raddio," mimicked Emil. He winked at Pearly, recovered from her fright but solemnly watchful; shouting assurance into his grandfather's ear, he shunted him through the curtain.

Pearly could hear them banging in the next room. She smoothed her skirt at the hips and, after a little wiggle, defied the emptiness. Scattered potatoes caught her eye and these she gathered hastily and restored to the bin. Beyond the curtain the bad words Grandfather Gillibo was saying made her giggle but renewed that breathless feeling in her chest. When she had strolled to the candy case she could still hear him, but she did not hear Emil till the whisper of his stride stopped at her back.

"Old fool," said Emil. "It's burnt out."

He was twice her height and, that close, shadowed by the light behind him, his eyelids drooped and only a glint of tooth to show that he smiled, he seemed, when she turned, to blanket her in darkness. With his black hair and his sallow skin he was dark at any time, but now he smelled dark, like the night.

He said, "You want some candy?"

Pearly nodded. She watched one of Emil's hands, flat to his thighs, rise slowly. He opened it as if he were puzzled to find it clenched, as if he were surprised by the wad of paper in the palm. When the paper slid to the floor he did not try to catch it; he let it fall and did not close his spread fingers while his cheeks sucked in and out. She hoped, conciliatingly, he wasn't mad about the potatoes.

Emil said, "Look—you want some real good candy?"

"I ain't got no more money."

"That don't matter. This is—city candy. It's upstairs."

A little silence fell which Emil broke, not looking at her.

"She's gone. You needn't to be afraid."

Pearly said, "How about him?"

"He don't matter. He can't hear."

All at once Emil touched her shoulder and took his hand away quickly and walked to the foot of the stairs.

"C'mon," he urged.

Pearly looked at the chocolate bars. She looked at the curtain. Smoothing her hips, she followed Emil up the stairs.

The room was the cleanest she had ever seen. And the barest. There were two beds in it and a bureau with a lighted lamp on it and a chair and a trunk. But, except for a long gun across one of the beds, no truck at all. When Emil sat on the other bed and pulled her to him she didn't resist; she waited passively, pressed to his darkness, to his curious, dark smell.

Emil seemed to be waiting, too, and after a little, when nothing more happened, she giggled. She felt his clasp weaken. She backed away; Emil had begun to tremble.

He stayed on the bed shaking and scrunched together as if he believed she was going to hit him, and as she stared in wonder suddenly the giggles got her, rocking her back and forth in spasms of glee.

"Don't you laugh!" he gasped suddenly. "Don't you laugh at me!"

But Pearly could not stop. And even when she was on the road again laughter returned at intervals so that she must lie in the grass, panting and giggling as she had before she rushed down the stairs, when Emil just huddled there, his hands covering his eyes.

CHAPTER TEN
THE TAPROOM

MINE HOST FELIXIO, the genial boniface, so by the local press acclaimed, recognized one of those moments in which the soul rejoiceth. As in the days of Simon, when every man sat under his vine and fig tree with none to fray him, Felixio basked beneath a roof without a mortgage, amid possessions glorious—buck's head—and useful—cash register—while Science, by permission of Bulova and the copyright owners; Art, bottled under government supervision, and Time, yet forty minutes from closing, inspired the peasants and patricians of a great democracy to amiable extravagance for his ultimate good. Like Noah, cozy within his ark above the raging flood, Felixio praised the Lord and blessed His creatures, including those awful dog.

Now, fluttering to the setter, the dove offered an olive branch.

"Sweet—sweet," cooed Beatrice above the couched head. So her murmur fell on Felixio, on fuddled Havla, enamored Perry Titcomb and, at the neighboring table, Joe Purdy, distracted thereby from consideration of another beer. For Beatrice made a sweet picture where, past her smooth cheeks, the Dutch bob cascaded and the dog lifted sad eyes to her entreaty.

Even Havla woke from his stupor. "You like?"

The bob assented gravely. "He's sweet. What's his name?"

"Ain't got no name. Him bitch."

"Ooooo," murmured Beatrice, fondling the silky ears. Havla suppressed a growl on his other side while the setter shivered under her touch.

To Stone, coming up from the rear, the spectacle of suppliant youth must have been not without attraction, but he bent his scrutiny beyond her, his booted legs spread, his chin on his chest like a judge at a bench show, his crop dangling from his hip. Though the setter's tail began to thrash, the shivering did not slacken.

After a minute, "What's the matter with that animal?" demanded Stone. "Distemper?"

Havla shook his head violently. "No, no! She good dog!"

"She's no good for birds, I'll bet."

Selena looked up. She had been slowly twisting the glass in front of her as if, for her lips seemed pleased, some pleasant secret preoccupied her, or as if she sought to prove that she could rotate the beer without spilling it, or perhaps for no purpose, the idle twirl of one for whom time and thought have paused in a small circle of contentment.

"No, no," declared Havla. "She good bird dog. She——"

"Don't try to kid me," interrupted Stone. "I know dogs. Her head's too small. She's got no nose. She'd be lousy on birds."

The spectators glanced from Beatrice to Stone and back to Beatrice—save Selena, who fixed her eyes on Joe, and Felixio; mine host, tipping his chair, laced his fingers across his stomach and took issue with authority.

"Lousay!" he exploded. "So you say, Meester Stone. And how you know? How you say lousay?"

"Look at her shake." The quiver continued despite the thrashing tail. "That dog's felt bird shot instead of the whip. Nevertheless"—Stone wheeled on Havla—"I could use a bitch. What 'll you take for her, old man?"

Havla chuckled. "No whip *her*—whip *him!*"

His prodding foot drew a rumble, and Havla cuffed the huge ugly head, and Stone laughed.

"Okay, old man—you whip that brute—I'll teach the bitch. Ten dollars! What do you say?"

Havla licked his lips. The rest were silent, watchful. Selena raised her glass and over its rim her eyes changed a little; not apprehension but a calm wariness regarded Joe. One of his ears, between her and the light, glowed red to the tip.

"No sell dog," said Havla huskily. Then a number of things happened. Beatrice rose, her pretty gesture resigning bargaining to the men. Stone stepped forward, stooping where she had knelt, saying, "Let's see those teeth," as Felixio crowed a high hee-hee and let his chair drop. Its sudden thump preceded by seconds Stone's grip on the setter's jaw, the setter's quick whine and a snarling roar that drowned everything but Beatrice's scream. Hurtling fury knocked Havla sidewise and Stone was down, lashing desperately with his crop.

Gunderson vaulted the bar. He went in low and hard like a blocking halfback. So did Joe Purdy; so did Havla; the whirl of men and animals became almost comic, a slice of a Popeye movie. When it cleared Havla and Joe held the raging mongrel; the setter cowered against the wall; Gunderson was dragging Stone to his feet; Felixio had made himself small behind a table; Beatrice clung to Perry Titcomb, and the taproom boiled with those rushing up and those scrambling away. Only Selena sat where she was, unagitated except to clutch the toppling beers.

Said John Faith, between Gunderson and Stone, "What happened?"

"Ask him," said Gunderson with a jerk of the head.

Stone's lungs heaved. His eyes glared at his fists clenched on the crop. The backs of his hands were bloody.

"I'll tell you what happened," panted Stone. "That"—he panted—"hellhound"—he panted—"jumped me!"

Felixio jabbered, "Meester Stone!—please!—is ladies here——" as Stone raised the crop.

The crop struck.

The big dog snapped, snarled, pawed with mad feet.

The crop struck again.

"Stop, you fool!" cried Gunderson.

Joe Purdy had shouted high and unintelligibly. He twisted both hands in the writhing dog's collar and hauled from his heels, his eyes blazing.

"I'll turn him loose," he warned in the cracking voice of adolescence. "I'll turn him loose!"

In a long discordant minor the record on the nickelodeon ran out, leaving the hush to choked snarls and the whimper of the setter. Stone's face was demonic. Only Gunderson's hammerlock across his throat separated the madman and the wolf.

John Faith's drawl may have been a shade less deliberate than usual. "You better get those bites cauterized—if you been bit. Some iodine anyway. Doc McKasker was here awhile ago. If he's gone, we'll roust him out and make him open up for us. Come on, Mr Stone."

Stone's glare fell again to the fists now dripping blood steadily; all his muscles seemed to wilt and, as Gunderson took the crop, he turned without a word and went out with Faith's hand on his elbow. The drawl came back—"was a fellow over by Clinton got bit in the belly once"—and the closing door released the hubbub.

His peace blasted, his glory brought low, his snug harbor swept by the hurricanes of passion, Felixio, gesticulating, ranting, calling alternately on heaven and hell, ordered Havla to get out. Around them surged the winds of advice. It was the guy's fault. It was the girl's fault. She should 've minded her own business. He oughtn't 've butted in. Sure, put the old boy out before the guy gets back. Better wait. Report the dog. Phone the troopers. Shucks, Felixio, you started it or your chair did!

Re-entrenched behind the bar, Gunderson listened to opinions rain on one little man a safe distance from peril and another at bay with his dogs, and reflected that he would write Svenson tomorrow to get his old job back. Women! Great god on a mountain, they could cause more trouble than a hornet in a backhouse!

He'd sooner scrub eunuchs till his arm fell off than work around women and liquor; put those two together and you might as well call the wagon, and if there was dogs in it, so much the worse. Love me love my dog, they said, and if you did or you didn't, you wound up behind the eight ball. Like that little hotpants running back to the booth—and how in hell did a swell woman like Mrs Danby draw that?—grinning like she'd hit the jackpot and leaving behind her, just because she had to pet the darling little doggie, one hell of a mess for him and Felixio and Stone and God knows who else. Not that he gave a damn about Stone. It was too bad that young fellow hadn't turned loose Butch to chaw Stone's ears off.

The young fellow had gone back to his table where he sat dazedly, his head down, a hand thrust into his disordered hair. The woman leaned forward and touched him.

"Look," said Selena, "look, Joe—there's nothing to feel bad about. Drink your beer," she urged. "You ain't done nothing."

He sat erect and she saw his eyes again, the wild look draining out and in its place confusion and appeal and hurt. She smiled at him.

"I guess you're pretty quick, though, when you want to be. I declare I never saw anything quicker than the way you went all of a sudden. Did you think he was after the girl?"

Joe Purdy shook his head.

"Why didn't you grab her 'stead of the dog?" she said. "That was your chance. You let the other fellow beat you to it."

"But it wasn't her," explained Joe. "It was the dog."

She still smiled, but the smile was a little shaky; in the solemn blue of his eyes she could see it reflected.

"It was the dog," he said earnestly. "I know that dog; he's mean. But that fellow ought not to 've hit him!"

Selena did not drop her gaze, but something went out of it and he saw something else, which he could not understand, come in. He did not try to figure what it was.

"He oughtn't to 've hit him, Selena! I don't mean the way you think, because he was a fool and might have got bad hurt. I mean he just oughtn't. It was mean! He's meaner than that dog's mean, that fellow. I couldn't stand it, Selena, when he hit him!"

She looked away and then, as the noise around Felixio stilled, withdrew her hand and pressed the back of his.

"They're going," she said, directing his attention with a nod.

Mrs Danby and some others were approaching the bar. Mrs Danby had received gratefully Trimble's suggestion that they leave. She had not cried out when it happened or lost her temper or even her composure. Once a liner she was on had rammed a smaller ship, a tanker, off Calais, and when all the passengers were rushing about and she was leaning over the boat-deck rail, watching in fascinated horror the crew of the sinking tanker leap for the liner's lower deck and some of them miss and go down between the grinding ships, a man had seized her shoulder and shouted at her to put on a life belt and she had been startled to discover everyone else in life belts and had scampered to her cabin where Danby, who was not sober, struggled with his and taken humbly his calling her a dumb idiot and been rather ashamed for being more interested in witnessing death than in saving her own life. She had known ever since that poise was no acquired nobility but something you either had or you hadn't and probably merely an incapacity to feel, indicating a shallow nature, so when the dog bit Bibby, if that was what the dog was doing, and her immediate reaction was a flash that Bibby must have had it coming to her she was ashamed of her serenity and got up and, with unusual solicitude, asked the child if she was all right. Quite all right, Bibby had said, snuggling her young man's arm, and Mrs Danby had thought, Oh dear, she's going to make a hero of him and he is so very redheaded and her mother will never forgive me. So when Trimble said, "Let's get out of this," she had agreed with alacrity.

Yet relief—relief that Bibby wasn't bitten, relief at going—by no means predominated in Mrs Danby. She assured herself that she was glad to go, had wanted for some time to go, ever since Rodney began to get whimsical or from the moment Stone joined them or perhaps at the end of John Faith's story; anyway, at that instant in the evening when a quality went out of it, an excitement, an anticipation, leaving it dull and a trifle sordid and urgently to be rid of, like a piece of bad meat in one's icebox. The row had finished things, a fitting climax to disenchantment and a fine excuse for abrupt departure. And yet, and yet, this other self rebelled; this self that was forever contrary, forever questing, laughing at conventions, whispering to her that something was not finished, leading her eternally to boat rails and urging that she peer over them and forget the life belts.

Stay, invited this other self; he's coming back.

Hell—thought Mrs Danby—all these emotions! She all but stamped her foot at Rodney.

Rodney was being difficult. Rodney demanded to know what had happened and what hath man of all his labor; life, asserted Rodney loudly, was muck, muck; but the artist wherever—wherever! he proclaimed—could build his ivory tower. Rodney grinned from its battlements, his own gargoyle.

"Won't somebody?" appealed Mrs Danby. "Mr——?"

"Titcomb," said the redheaded young man and obligingly made himself a derrick. So, with Rodney protesting but lugged regardless, the young man followed Trimble, who followed Mrs Danby, who led the way with one arm around Beatrice in what, she felt, was an absurdly motherly attitude, as if she were marching in a pageant or they were about to do charades.

To them Felixio darted, halting the procession.

"Mrs Danby!—I am so sorry——"

She began to regret in earnest now, with so many eyes upon her and Felixio fluttering and fawning, that she was not out of it, and when from somewhere a Negro in a chauffeur's cap appeared and Trimble said Laurence would drive them home she marveled at her vacillation. But no—she had her own car—it was kind of him, but——

"Rum!" croaked Rodney. "Rum—rum— rum——

"—but if you could do something about *that!*"

Trimble spoke to the Negro and in a moment the Negro was no longer there and neither was Rodney nor the redheaded young man, and only her niece, pouting but beginning to inspect the remaining baseball players, weighed on Mrs Danby's conscience. All at once Mrs Danby made a decision. She had been aware, throughout Felixio's apologies and amid all the other stares, of the woman's. The woman sat a few feet away in a blue-and-white print and a white straw hat with grapes on it and Mrs Danby's first thought was that the dress was homemade and nobody had worn hats like that for five years. Her second was that this was the woman Trimble knew; she was his neighbor, Trimble had said. Then her gaze met the woman's and an old distress stirred in its sleep. She was being looked at, Mrs Danby realized, as she imagined girls in shops sometimes looked at her, with envy and some malice and a good deal of wistfulness—the look a five-and-dime girl might turn on Barbara Hutton. "If I were only you," the look said, "but if I were, how much lovelier, how much happier——" And Mrs Danby, meeting the look, thought as she had sometimes thought before, " 'There but for the grace of God——' " and wished a little sadly that God had been less gracious. All right, she wanted to say to the woman, the hat came from Suzy and the coat from Bergdorf, but they are not going to stay in a barroom and have fun; they are going home with a drunken egotist and a niece who is twenty years younger than I am and they will never, never know fun in all their lives.

It was over quickly; the woman looked away; Mrs Danby dropped her arm from Bibby's waist and touched Bibby's shoulder.

"Darling, run along with them. I'll follow in my car."

"But, Aunt Gretchen——"

"Please—I'm not up to arguing now. Mr Trimble, won't you please——"

"Of course," said Trimble.

When they had gone Mrs Danby crooked a finger at Gunderson.

"Bill," she told him, when she had returned to the booth, "I want a double scotch and soda."

And that, Selena guessed, is the woman Jack Faith used to mention when he would come by the store at odd times and sit and gas by the hour, until Emil was half nuts dodging out and dodging in "to catch him at his tricks." She never could make up her mind whether Jack Faith hung around just to plague Emil or because he was lonely or to make a real play for her like his friend, Harvey Slope, had. Anyway, it didn't matter; she didn't want any part of either of them, then or ever. But it had been sort of nice hearing somebody talk about something besides fertilizers and funerals, and sometimes he had talked poetry to her, and she herself had talked an awful lot too. One thing she was sure of: in Jack Faith's opinion Mrs Russell Danby was about the swellest woman that lived.

"Do you know her?" she asked Joe, and when he shook his head she said, "She owns that big place on the right coming into Madison, used to be part of the Fernleigh farms. I think her husband's dead or divorced or something; anyway, he's never around. Do you think she's pretty, Joe?"

"I never noticed," Joe said.

"You noticed the girl. You think she's pretty, don't you?"

Joe started a nod and checked it and started a shake of his head and checked that too. His eyes had that funny, desperate light they had when he came into the store tonight.

"I think——" Joe said and stopped.

"What?" said Selena.

"I think——"

He couldn't say words like that. They would sound soppy. And if he did, she would laugh at him; she was going to laugh at him anyway, he guessed.

But Selena didn't laugh. She didn't do anything and she didn't say anything; she just looked at him, and though he wanted to keep on looking at her, because he meant what he was about to say and because he wanted her to know it and because, doggit, he wanted to look at her, he must look instead at the table, his hand with the knuckles torn where he had scrabbled on the floor, while one thought burned through his head—the way she was. The way she was back there in the store when he suddenly opened up; the way she was on the road, listening, talking; the way she was here. He had no other phrase for it, but it was enough to fill him.

"Aw, gee, Joe," said Selena slowly, and now he didn't mind her smile, "don't be blue. Those people don't matter. The fight didn't matter. It wasn't any of your doing. We were having a good time. You know? Like we said back there in the car—somebody to talk to, someplace to go; nothing to worry about much. I'm having a good time. Aren't you, Joe?"

He lifted his face and laughter broke across it.

"Yeah," he confessed. The door opened and Stone entered with John Faith.

There were bandages on both Stone's hands and a strip of court plaster along one cheek. There were stains on his shirt and his corduroy trousers, a rip in the shiny leather of one boot, but his face had been washed and his hair combed back and there was nothing cocky about him save his cocky stride. Nevertheless, the taproom went as still as a church.

John Faith dropped back a step; in the twist of his mouth was the resignation of a man who has lost an argument. He glanced toward the booth and waved cavalierly, but he did not go to Mrs Danby at once.

Stone stopped at the bar.

"My crop, please," he said dourly. Gunderson looked dubious. "Don't worry," said Stone. "I'm not going to hit anybody. Or anything," he added. Gunderson handed him the crop.

From the nearest group Felixio stepped. "Meester Stone——"

"Just a minute!"

His gesture was theatrical and, as he faced the corner where Havla crouched, Stone seemed to make the room a stage and himself an actor who has rehearsed a part and will brook no interference with its delivery.

"Will you sell that setter?" he called.

Sometime before Havla had retired to the space between the skeeball game and the wall whence he could peer at the jury debating his fate while he shepherded the dogs from sight. Only his shoulders, his battered hat and his knob of a chin projected above the wooden runway. From where she sat Mrs Danby could barely see him. He reminded her of a picture in the newspapers at the time of the great radio scare, of an old Jersey farmer behind his wood-pile resolved to sell his life dearly to the men from Mars.

"Can't he let him alone?" she said as John Faith came up. But Faith put out his hand as if to hush her.

At the sound of Stone's voice the taproom had begun reverberating with continuous guttural rumbles. Stone waited. If he was afraid, only his glistening temples showed it.

"Meester Stone——" begged Felixio.

"Because if you won't," called Stone, "I'm going to report that brute and have him shot. Sell me the setter and I'll call it quits."

The knob of chin under the scarecrow's hat did not move.

A murmur rose.

"Hell—sell him the setter!" shrilled a voice. "What good's a dead dog when you can git money for a live one?"

Several men guffawed and the hero of the quip could be heard repeating it with self-appreciative chuckles until the murmur subsided and the crowd was quiet again, all the faces toward

Havla. Mrs Danby felt a little sick, for now something enveloped the room that was harsh and callous and bluntly masculine.

"Can't you stop it?" she whispered. But Faith already was going away from her, walking swiftly and lightly around Stone, around Felixio and the others to the table where the woman sat.

"I'll give you fifty dollars," called Stone.

When Havla did not answer he shoved a bandaged hand into his pocket and gingerly waved a roll of bills.

"Fifty dollars," he taunted. "Fifty dollars for a gun-shy set-ter—or else!"

Through the bloodbeat in his ears, as if from a long way off, Joe heard another voice, whispering, urgent, persistent—"Don't, Joe, don't; it ain't none of your business, Joe"—like conscience crying under rolling fathoms of desire, and he knew, though his arms registered no sensation save the muscles tightening until they trembled, that a hand gripped them and that the hand belonged to the voice and both to Selena.

Suddenly Havla spoke in a short, clipped singsong.

"Okay—you come get setter."

Stone hesitated; obviously the next move was his. A man snickered and for an instant tension hung on the brink of shat-tering laughter. Gunderson, stalking out, checked the wave.

"Give me that fifty bucks."

Mechanically Stone handed him five tens.

"The only reason I'm doing this," said Gunderson, "is not to help you, sportsman, but to get you the hell out of here."

Stone's face was malignant. "See here——"

"You, Gunderson——" piped Felixio.

"Shut up, the both of you!"

The big man walked toward Havla.

"Put her up here."

Lifted, pushed, whimpering, the setter came scrambling over the guardrail onto the skeeball trough. Gunderson gathered her under one arm, tossed the money on the trough and walked away while Havla, fighting the other dog back, fumbled for the bills.

"Here's your pooch." Gunderson dropped the setter at Stone's feet, tossed him the leash. "Now scram, sportsman!"

Stone missed the leash and stooped and retrieved it while the setter groveled. They watched him as they had watched Havla a little while before, and Mrs Danby fancied she could hear their hard breathing above her own.

"My dog?" sneered Stone at large. He jerked the leash. "So he never whipped you, eh?"

From beyond the bystanders John Faith's voice pleaded— "Easy, boy, easy. He's paid for the dog. It's his dog now."

Stone paused at the door.

"Goodnight, gentlemen!" The crop whisked the air as though he tested its resilience. He spoke to the setter, "Come on, my dog."

He laughed and went out, dragging the setter at his heels.

For a long time to come, whenever she saw a dog, whether trotting along a highway or promenading Park Avenue, Mrs Danby was to remember this evening and was to drive away the reproach that she might have done something. If she had interfered in some way; if she had cajoled Stone or bossed him or outbid him; if she had defied him and used local influence; if she had chosen any course but dumb disgust; if—— The dog would trot out of sight and Mrs Danby slowly would forget the pain and the fact that, on this evening, she had done nothing but be a lady, sitting supinely until it was over, until Stone had gone and everybody was talking at once, and the old man had lurched out, and Felixio was firing Bill, and John Faith, instead of rushing to reassure her, stayed at the table of Trimble's neighbor, that woman whose hats were five years old but whose eyes were strange.

"I'm disappointed in you," she told him when he finally came to her. "Surely you could have stopped him."

"Stone? No—I tried outside. He had a fixed idea. I don't think he knows himself exactly who he's doing it to—the dogs, Havla, all of us, society—but he was busting for revenge and I guess he'll get it."

"Do you mean——"

She stopped at the somberness of his face.

John Faith said quietly, "Not necessarily. They don't as a race like dogs and they're terribly frustrated, for which you can't much blame them. But they're more the other thing than they are sadistic. I wasn't worried about the setter; I was worried about young Purdy."

"Purdy?"

"Kid that held the big dog, almost turned him loose. Most country boys are pretty indifferent to dogs, but Joe's not like most country boys. He loves the country. And when that fellow bought the setter I was afraid he was going for him."

"What did you do?"

"Well, we talked to him," said John Faith.

They talked to him, Mr Faith pressing him into the chair and Selena hanging onto his arm. Don't be a damn fool, Joe; you can't stop him from buying the dog and you can't stop him from beating the dog once he owns it. What's it going to get you knocking his block off? You'll only get in big trouble. He'll call the troopers or Felixio will and they'll run you in and you've got your father to think about, Joe, and your mother. What 'll they say if you get pinched in a drunken brawl?

"I ain't drunk, Mr Faith."

I know you're not, but how will they know it? They won't understand, will they, if you tell 'em you got pinched because you didn't like a guy for buying a dog and one of Havla's dogs at that? Hell, Joe, I feel like you do but there ain't much to be done about it and this ain't the place to do it in. Hold your horses—you and me 'll catch this guy on a back road on a dark night and make him sorry.

Mr Faith was grinning at him, so he grinned at Mr Faith and said again, "Honest, I ain't drunk."

"Okay"—said Mr Faith—"but I never saw a guy so scrappy on ice water; what got into you, boy?"

"I guess it was the sun; you know, in my sap at the end of the day."

He must have looked pretty sheepish when he said that, because Mr Faith laughed and looked at him with that kidding look in his eye and sat down and said he would like to buy them a drink. The fellow was gone by then and old man Havla, too, and everybody was too busy talking to everybody else to pay any attention to them.

"All right," he said to Mr Faith.

Selena said, "I don't want a drink."

It came to him that this was the first thing Selena had said in quite a while and it came to him, too, that he was hanging onto her hand. That came to him because, suddenly, she took it away. He looked at her and saw that she was looking at Mr Faith in that way she always looked at people in the store.

Mr Faith got up. He stood with his hands in his pockets and his head cocked on one side, looking down at both of them.

"Why not, Mrs Gillibo?" he said. "Ah, make the most of what we yet may spend before we too—— Yes! I think you should have a drink. I'll tell Bill to send them over."

He went away and pretty soon two drinks came. Mr Faith didn't come back. They didn't say anything. They drank their drinks. When Selena put hers down she reached across the table and got her hand under his and he held onto it. They were sitting like that when people began to go out of the place and the boss of the place yelled that it was time to close up.

CHAPTER ELEVEN
THE ROAD

THE BIG CLOCK in front of Valley Service said eleven twenty-five when a police car, going west, passed the traffic signal, made a leisurely U turn and stopped in the shadow of an elm directly across from Valley Inn. A state trooper got out and walked to the service station where he entered the refreshment stand. While the trooper in the car waited two men left the Inn and disappeared, walking rapidly, in the direction of the town. The trooper in the car could see them clearly across the intervening highway, for though the Inn's gables were sunk into the black sky, a strong light bathed the long old-fashioned veranda and the row of automobiles parked head on against it.

"They say he's there," said the returning trooper.

"I know; I recognize his car. And his pal left a minute ago with another guy. We can take our time."

The speaker shook out cigarettes and both troopers settled on their spines and smoked with a minimum of conversation. Darkness and quiet held the countryside except for the road running through it like a clock's tick through sleep. Occasional cars passed. By dawn traffic would increase. A bus, luminous in gold and red and green, rolled in from the west, its passengers too vitiated by heat and dust and the protracted end to holiday to lift their heads. The bus refueled and rolled on. One of the troopers nudged the other; a car had turned off the highway and drawn up at the Inn.

"Looks like Jack Faith's," said the trooper. "That's funny."

A Negro chauffeur had gotten out of the car. He stood for a moment listening to the buzz of voices from the open windows and then went up the steps. Presently he reappeared. Now he supported on one side a man obviously drunk who was supported on the other by a baseball player in uniform. An argument ensued. The drunk wanted another drink; the baseball player was trying to get him to go with the chauffeur; they might, to the audience under the elm, have been a trio in a vaudeville show.

The baseball player won. By main force, though still in coaxing tones, he boosted his charge into the back of a black sedan while the chauffeur climbed into the front. This was not the car in which the chauffeur had arrived, but evidently he was at home. His glum face leaned out from the wheel and his query came plaintive across the gravel.

"But where at do he live?"

The baseball player made impatient signs. "First house on the left when you pass the intersection. Big house on a hill. You can't miss it!"

"But supposin' he won't git out. Is they anybody——"

From the back of the sedan floated a wavering effort at song.

"Roll—out—the barrel——"

"Go wan, go wan!" snarled the baseball player.

Said one trooper to the other, "That must be Mrs Danby's place he's talking about."

"Yeah. She's inside, too, I guess."

"Where does she get them screw balls? Hell, a woman like her can have who she pleases, but always it's screw balls she gets. I remember last summer——"

"Get a load of this," said the other trooper.

Down the steps skimmed a girl, bareheaded, trailing a white sports coat and in every respect, even at forty yards in a bad light, an eyeful.

"Oh boy!" exclaimed a trooper.

The baseball player turned, raising his hands, and the girl halted as if, were these spears, she might choose to die on them. So they stood looking at one another, their words drowned in the noise of the departing sedan and neither paying attention to the man who had followed the girl and who hesitated now, a tall figure in white linen, on the bottom step.

Suddenly the girl called, "Goodnight, Mr Trimble! Don't you bother about me. Perry 'll take me home!"

The troopers saw two get into a cut-down Ford, heard a laugh killed by the explosion of an engine and watched a second tail-light disappear eastward.

"Perry's got his."

"I'll say. Boy, you and me chasing the wrong fox."

The troopers resumed their vigil over the Inn. The man in white linen had not altered his aimless position, one foot advanced as if he deliberated whether to go on or go back. He finally decided to do neither; he sat on the bottom step and lit a cigarette. The troopers also smoked. Two cars passed.

A third car, coming from the west in a splutter of ancient mechanism, stopped near the service station. A moment later its driver crossed the road. He was another tall man, but as he entered the flood of light where the man in linen sat he looked dingy by comparison, from the straw hat on the back of his head to his dragging feet. The troopers saw him approach the Inn's steps and then delay as if he had but just noticed the seated man. This one got up and spoke and the other answered. Their voices fell indistinct and unimportant, something about the hot night, something about who was in the Inn. The troopers started discussing how long it would be before midnight.

Leadheels and the man in linen concluded their remarks; evidently Leadheels had changed his mind and decided not to have a nightcap. He recrossed the road, pausing once to call back. "You ain't seen me, see? You know how 'tis when a feller's stepping out!" His laugh hung high and nervous in the hot night until the man in linen nodded; then he dragged on.

"Look what's coming; that guy's been in a wreck."

The trooper at the wheel shook his head.

"Ain't possible. That's the guy left a minute ago with Faith. He wasn't bandaged then."

"He's plenty bandaged now. Both hands. Maybe he socked Faith. I always said that fellow Faith had a hard head!"

Cackling, they watched two men stride up the steps and the man in linen, who had risen again but who did not accompany them into the Inn, begin pacing up and down. The troopers had forgotten Leadheels; now their attention was diverted to him. Leadheels was having trouble with his car: he tried the starter—nothing happened; he tried again; he got out and cursed and raised the hood.

"Why'n't you crank her, bud?" called the humorous trooper. The other trooper paid him the tribute of his mirth.

Leadheels straightened. Faint light from the Inn, obliquely striking the straw hat and gaunt face, gave him a comically sinister air. All at once he shook his fist.

"Don't you laugh at me! You hear? Don't you laugh!"

The law was no more prepared for this outburst than for doomsday. Startled, the troopers did nothing while Leadheels, trembling visibly even at a distance, fell to his tinkering.

"Why, the son of a bitch," said the humorous trooper. "Let's run him in."

"Aw, nuts to him," said the trooper at the wheel. "It's that poor heel from over by Little Salem. He's half nuts anyway."

"Let's pull him anyway."

"And miss the other fellow? Nothing doing."

"Okay. But I'm getting tired of this. Call me when breakfast's ready."

He hung his legs over the door of the car and slumped to his neck with his cap down on his eyes. The trooper at the wheel lit another cigarette. From time to time he informed his companion.

"He got her started ... but he didn't go far. Musta broke down again. ... Here comes somebody from the Inn. It's the fellow with the bum dukes. He's got a dog with him."

"Dunno how a fellow can drive in that fix."

"He drove all right. ... Place must be fulla dogs. Here comes another fellow with a dog. And boy, is he drunk!"

"Him or the dog?"

"Him."

"Let's run him in then."

"Is that all you can think about? You must love spending your time off in court. He'll make it ... if him or the dog don't kill each other first. Hear 'em?"

A crescendo of violent sound passed.

"Lucky thing he ain't going the same way as the other fellow," commented the tired trooper. "Make a nice mess picking dog assholes from human."

"The nigger's back," said the trooper at the wheel.

His partner hoisted himself to watch the Packard roll in and the man in linen roll away.

"Pretty soft. Who's he?"

"Never saw him before. Must be one of them city farmers. What time is it?"

"Must be pretty near closing time. Uh-huh. Here they come."

Out of the Inn, in groups and pairs on a surge of talk and laughter, dribbled Felixio's customers. For most of them the evening was done. They had hunted holiday down; they had washed it up and stowed it away; dutifully they had sidetracked duty to pleasure and for a little while excitement had captured them. Now they were fain to beg quits. Here and there a Mayhew, willy-nilly, would endure anguish into the night and doubtless into the days, and tomorrow the behavior of a Titcomb would become county gossip. But already, at midnight, the sun of regularity was rising here.

The troopers heard the good-byes called. They watched the cars drum out, east or west, toward the back roads and the byways curling into the Hunterdon Hills, until only a few stood silent and unclaimed. Within the Inn music stopped in the middle of a bar. A lighted window went dark. The last revelers, a couple, drew close together before they, too, took the highway west.

"Hell," said a trooper, "he didn't come out."

"But they swore he was there."

"And his car's still there, ain't it?"

As they spoke the door of the Inn, which someone had closed with a rasp of locks and bolts, reopened and a figure, elfin but grandiose, emerged. If the editor of the Madison *Gazette* was being ejected he betrayed no mortification. Empirically Slope paused to scan the field before, ignoring the lurking foe, he swayed to his chariot.

"Did he see us?"

"Hell, he's so drunk he can't see his own windshield. Let's get him."

The Packard ran mighty sweet after that Chevrolet. If he had to hunt him a job next winter maybe he could get aholt of an old Packard and run his own taxi. Maybe he could get aholt of this one. Mr Trimble didn't know much about cars. Maybe if Mr Trimble took a hate to this one; if something happened to it and kept happening, maybe Mr Trimble would trade it in cheap. Maybe he'd get so mad he'd just naturally give it away, like that time down in Virginia when he was a caddy and that white man got so mad he give away all his clubs what he didn't bust on the tree. Man, oh man!

"Drive slower, Laurence."

"Yas, suh."

Yas, suh, Mr Trimble, we'll keep it down long as you in the back. When you ain't it's hello, seventy! But that was two cops back yonder; better keep it down anyhow. They was laying for somebody. He'd seen 'em when he first drove up, before they brought out the drunk gentleman, and he'd been mighty careful all the way out to that place and back. The drunk gentleman had looked like he might be a handful the way he was singing and carrying on, and such talk! Wild talk. Like they had him in jail and if he ever bust out he was going to fix 'em like Samson fix those folks in the Bible. He called 'em by the same name those folks was called and a heap worse. Would you like the radio, he had asked the gentleman, and the gentleman had said, If you dare to play that some'n' of civilization, I shall personally nail you to the cross where me and genius have been crucified. Wild talk! So he didn't play nothing, even though it was pretty near time for the Cotton Club. He helped the gentleman out when they got to where they was going and it was a big house, a fine house, with nobody in sight; but the gentleman by that time, thank Jesus, was most passed out, so all he had to do was lay him on a rug in the front room and light out from there. He switched on the radio almost before he switched on the ignition and it was Cab Calloway. He'd be hearing him yet if it hadn't been for picking up Mr Trimble and getting back on that goddamn hill. I got Harlem on my mind; man, oh man!

Drive slower, Laurence, he had cautioned, mistrusting the darkness, mistrusting the road, mistrusting most of all the maniac who might chance out of nowhere; drive slower or by chance he will smash you. Yet with all his heart he longed for speed; speed to escape, speed to hasten security, speed to get home.

And how compellingly he thought of it as "home" when but awhile ago he had so lightly given up its new-flagged hearth. But since then, he paraphrased to himself, I have eaten vetch and am no longer a golden tramp.

Vetch—people; more especially, women. They were, in truth, ineradicable as weeds. Pretty women, plain women, ingénues, garrulous old gossips, little girls; since morning they had been thrown at him no matter how gratefully he would have done without the sex.

I do not like women, he thought. I do not like their prying, their snuggling and their twining; I do not like their femaleness. They are predatory and possessive; they are crows. All the time I was talking to the boy she was looking at me like a black-eyed crow; why should I not have told Gillibo outright that she was in there intent on deceiving him? Instead of lying about the boy. And that other one, making her bid for John so boldly, she is predatory, too, for all her lacquered smile.

"This is the hermit of Little Salem."

"Oh, but you mustn't! We lonely country women simply can't let our men be hermits," while her seeking eyes read him.

What was it Blackmore called them? The mothers of all mischief.

And he remembered that friend in town, in that tearoom where they were two men among a hundred women. "Look at them! Listen to them! There is something horrible about a swarm of women, don't you think? Something naked and indecent and merciless, like cannibals. Do you know what I would like to do? I would like to stand up and shout, 'Where are your men? I will tell you—they are all dead! They are dead, whether they walk or lie in their graves, and you have killed them!'"

Down among the dead men. John among the dead men. Gillibo among the dead men. And the boy? All among the dead men while women go on forever. That was a play once—*Women Go On Forever*—God knows how many years ago in the days when the city enthralled him. Plays and supper clubs, liquor and lacquer, mink and mistresses, women and Winchell and taxicabs and the latest quip in the *New Yorker*, the whole a comic court dancing, symbolic and superior, while the dead men slaved, yet a court of refuge of a kind, a protection of a kind, instead of flight through darkest Jersey with chance on the running board. And flight to what? A marble buried in a patch of earth? A ghost house lonely on the Barrens?

He shivered and words tumbled to his throat—faster, Laurence, faster, faster!—and almost at once he felt better, for the words amused him. You are exactly like the Red Queen in Alice, he thought and, thinking of Alice, thought of his other books, on his shelves, on his bedside table, waiting his pleasure silently, compliantly, but how deeply communicative, how warmly satisfying!

Foreboding left him at the turnoff, returning only briefly as they reached his lane. Havla's car was stopped in the road beyond. He saw the old man by the light of a rising moon and heard his whistle. From the house he sent Laurence back to inquire.

"He wasn't broke down," Laurence reported. "He was whistling for his dog."

Trimble looked up, puzzled.

"But I saw a dog with him."

"It was his other dog he was whistling for."

"That can't be," said Trimble. "He sold it."

The man must be drunk; Trimble gave it up and returned to De Profundis.

The jalopy was a mile out of Madison before either spoke; then Beatrice, looking straight ahead, said, "This isn't the way home."

He didn't answer; he just drove.

Beatrice said, still looking straight ahead, "Do you know what a mirage is?"

"What?"

"That's where the little man who wasn't there keeps his car."

"Do you know what a myth is?" she said.

"What?"

"That's the little girl who wasn't there."

"What's a fable?" said Beatrice a moment later.

"What?"

"That's where the little girl who wasn't there keeps her horse."

They were on a dirt road then. He steered the jalopy onto the shoulder, stopped and cut off the lights. Even though she lifted her chin, she could hardly see him in the darkness.

"Don't you think they're cute gags?" she said.

He said, "What's smooching?"

She had begun to shake her head before she remembered that he probably couldn't see her very well either.

"Wha——" she began.

But it really didn't make any difference whether he saw her or not.

Gunderson had emptied the contents of the bureau drawers onto the bed and was taking their stuff out of the closet when Sigrid came in. She watched him open the trunk and lift the tray to a chair and pack the heavier clothes. Her face was expressionless except for its stamp of utter fatigue. It was a long narrow face with hollows beneath the cheekbones. In the bar, when she was either chewing gum or smiling, these were not so marked, but here, passive in the sharp, harsh light, her face looked peaked, sad and white under the rouge.

When he went on packing without a glance at her she began to help him, putting small things into the tray and laying out her few dresses where he could reach them easily. He took them without a word and added them to the clothes in the trunk. The piles on the bed shrank rapidly.

"The New York bus has gone," Sigrid said at last.

"We'll take the first one in the morning."

She was holding a bottle which she had removed from the little row of toilet articles on the bureau, and when he spoke she did not immediately place it in the tray but smoothed it around and around while she watched him pressing down the pile in the trunk.

"That Mrs Danby," she said, "she always liked you, didn't she?"

Gunderson made a snorting noise into the trunk.

"You know I don't mean nothing," she said. "But I bet she'd give you a job on her place."

"Doing what? Taking care of her caretakers?"

Sigrid placed the bottle in the tray. She tapped down the tops of the other bottles and wedged them here and there among softer objects.

"Couldn't Mr Faith find you a job?"

Gunderson closed the tray and latched it and settled it into the trunk. He said, while he lowered the trunk's lid, "If Jack Faith knew of a job outside the CCC camp he'd grab it himself. What do you think all that gang of kids out there tonight are looking for—daisies?"

He pressed down the lid with his huge hands and, when the lid failed to close, made a fist and pounded it. Sigrid said nothing; watching him, her face retained its sad inertia.

Gunderson drew back and regarded the unclosed trunk. He turned around to sit on it.

"There ain't anybody living in that old house out by Siloam," said Sigrid, "since they foreclosed on them folks. It's got a nice patch of ground—and a brook. I bet if we asked somebody——"

The crash of the lock silenced her; it left a ringing silence in the room.

Gunderson got down from the trunk. He was sweating copiously. He wiped his hands on the seat of his trousers, wiped his forehead with his forearm and faced her with his upper lip drawn back.

"Quit it," he said, "quit it! You know it's no good."

She had not been looking at him and she did not now, keeping her eyes down toward her knotted fingers and her lashes down on her eyes so that her face ran from him. But while he glared at that tired, passive mold it seemed to break like a piece of glass hit by a pebble and all its boniness shivered into jelly.

Gunderson spoke hoarsely. "Come here, Mrs Gunderson!"—and she came, weeping, into his hard, wet chest.

This was the ripple that, from away up on the Barrens, you believed would be bright and crowded and full of things happening, like a city street, but which wasn't that way at all. When cars passed they came with a roar and a flash that took your breath away, and between cars the highway was so gray and lonesome you were afraid. That way was Madison and that way Pennsylvania, but miles of lonesome road lay between you and them, and back there was Little Salem and the lonesome way you had come. You didn't want to go back and you were afraid to go ahead, so you squatted by the sign at the turnoff and wished you were riding in the bus that passed with all the pretty lights and that was going somewhere.

You could see from here, looking toward Pennsylvania, a far light that didn't move and the other way, looking toward Madison, a flashing red light that was just a red dot from up on the Barrens. You didn't know what the still light was but you knew the red flash was Mike's Bar-B-Q and you knew who was in there because you had sneaked up and peeked through the window and your father wasn't. You picked some you knew by sight, a Monski and a Romerley and a Norton, but you were afraid Mike would tell if he caught you hanging around, so you sneaked back and hid behind the sign where the earth was scooped out and after a while you lay down and watched the highway half in hope and half in fear that somebody would come along.

But when somebody did come it was from the other way, from Little Salem, and the car was past you and rattling toward Madison before you knew it. And then you must have gone to sleep, hugging the warm dirt and dreaming a funny kind of running dream, because all of a sudden you started awake with a flash in your eyes and an awful fear of your father. The flash was gone in a second and the yells, too, dying away toward Little

Salem, and you guessed that a car turning off the highway had blinded you and that this was your father and he was drunk and cursing the dogs. While you still lay there, shivering, another car turned off, blinding you again.

Now you got up and began to run. Now you were honestly afraid. The light ahead soon left you and you were alone on the lonesome road and you began to sob, thinking of the bad time ahead and everything you had risked for nothing. So, when headlights from behind grew, you stopped to let them catch you whoever or whatever they were.

Pearly stood whittled in dazzling brilliance.

Someone she could not see asked if she wanted a lift. Someone laughed and there were whispers and another voice: "I ain't afraid of her old man."

"Get in," urged the first voice.

She walked out of the radiance, smoothing down her dress.

"I dunno," she said, close to the car. "How—how many are you?"

There had been the semblance of an argument outside the Inn. Mrs Danby had said nonsense, she was perfectly capable of driving herself and Faith had said he was sure of that but not so sure of himself. He said if she would drive his car as far as her place, the ride would sober him and he could then drive himself home. But why shouldn't I drive you home in my car, Mrs Danby proposed. That, said Faith, was impossible; no woman had ever driven him home; it would be humiliating enough if she drove herself home in his car. It sounds like the same thing to me, Mrs Danby said. It isn't, Faith said. They wound up by taking Faith's car and Faith driving.

"But I just happened to think," said Mrs Danby as they proceeded at a sedate gait, "how it's going to look to leave my car standing in front of the Inn all night. What will people say?"

"They will say you are having an affair with Felixio."

"But I don't want them to say it."

"Too late. It will be the scandal of the club car Monday morning."

"Those awful brokers! I don't want to have an affair with Felixio."

"A romantic foreigner?"

"No. When I have an affair," said Mrs Danby firmly, "it will be for like, if not for love, and I don't like Mr Felixio."

An imp within suggested that she add, "I like you." She quailed; heavens, she was behaving worse than Bibby! In the same blush it occurred to her that John Faith was simply making conversation and, since they left the Inn, had really not been thinking of her at all.

"Why haven't you?" the imp demanded aloud. "Am I as stupid as all that?"

"What?" said Faith.

"Nothing. I was merely wondering what men muse about when they talk drivel to ladies."

"I apologize. As a matter of fact I was bothered about something."

"And I intruded?"

"Oh, it's nothing personal—a car I noticed near the Inn."

"The troopers?"

"No; the troopers versus Slope and Faith is too old a feud to matter; they gave up trying to hang it on me long ago. It was another car. It got me bothered about a friend of mine."

He did not explain further and Mrs Danby was silent, a little offended and even more put out with herself for the state of mind that let her be offended. Oh well, tomorrow she could forget tonight and its curious unrest; tomorrow she could lose her futile introversions in various to-dos; her hair and her fingernails would resume importance, and hats, curtains, rose spray and house parties take proper supremacy over such moonshine as "Why am I alive?" In the meantime the man driving, who was so bothered about somebody else, need be of no bother to her.

"You are habitually concerned about your friends, aren't you?" she remarked sweetly.

"What makes you say that?"

"An observation. I don't often see you, but whenever I do you seem to be playing good Samaritan. And I hear things—nothing goes on, apparently, without John Faith."

"You are meaning to say that I'm a busybody and a meddler. I guess I am. It's from want of something better to do. I don't like to admit it, but that's the motive. I try to kid myself—to believe it's kindness, unselfishness, a burning interest in my fellow man— you know, Faith the student of human nature going about with good deeds in one hand and a microscope in the other—A Boy Scout Under Freud, so to speak. But it's no go. I can't even flatter myself that I give to get a glow for my ego. The truth is that I'm just killing other people's time because my own's run out on me."

He had spoken seriously and Mrs Danby said, almost in anger, "That's a silly way to talk! You sound like someone in a play or a book who's been given a year to live. Can't you ever be gay?"

"Yes, I think I can. Was I not gay tonight?"

"You were amusing. I like to hear you talk."

"But I was not gay?"

"Chance and lunacy and baby chicks are not very gay subjects."

Faith drove in silence. He said at last, "I thought that I was gay. It seemed to me this morning, when I woke up, that the world was a pretty bad place. That was partly hangover, but it was more than that; it was a conviction that nothing in it can possibly compensate for the job of living. Whatever Ecclesiastes says about the grave it is better than a place where all is vanity."

"You are not amusing now," said Mrs Danby.

"And then," said Faith, as if she had not spoken, "tonight I changed my mind. Tonight I felt gay."

"Why?"

"You."

The single, simple word caught her completely unprepared. From one who had seemed always to avoid her, it came so unexpectedly that it was shocking, almost in bad taste. She cried, as merrily as she could, "Why, Mr Faith, I never dreamed——!"

Faith stopped the car. He looked at her intently.

"You asked me a question and I was trying to be honest. I was trying to tell you that I don't think I'm much of a fellow. And now I'm trying to tell you that I think you are. I don't get the chance often. I think you're about the swellest woman I ever met."

"But——" began Mrs Danby and stopped in sheer embarrassment at the consequences she had boldly invited. They had come up the long drive to Greenfields and around the semicircle to the court with its neat shrubs, fountain and deck chairs looking, even in the darkness, a little too formal, a little too exactly what you would expect. A light burned in the living room, but Rodney and Beatrice must have gone to bed, and Mrs Danby devoutly hoped they had and did not care greatly if it was together.

"Look," she said, "there's the moon," and as it broke the fringe of maples and climbed the deep lawn, "Are there any moon dials? I've always thought a moon dial would be nicer than a sundial. It wouldn't seem so ruthless somehow."

Faith did not answer. He had killed his engine and, as she spoke, he faced ahead, his angular nose and chin sharp in the moonlight. She watched him through a veil of curiosity that had slipped across her pique.

"Look," she said again, "I'm sorry if I was nasty. Do you know that I know very little about you? I wish you'd tell me something sometime."

Faith said, "If you mean where I came from, who my people were, what I do and what I have done, it isn't very interesting and certainly not important. I used to think it was. I used to get pretty well steamed up about myself, my individuality, my career, my future, my happiness; I used to think about them to the exclusion of practically everything else and talk about them whenever the other fellow would stop talking about his. But I gradually cut it out. Not that I became less loquacious or more generous; I just got fed up with Faith. Oh, he's had a life—mostly good, some bad—and I suppose there will come a day when it will mean more to him than it does now. I mean sitting around in the sun in some place like St Petersburg, Florida, yarning with the other old men about the fights they fought and the women they won. Right now, thank God, I'm a ways from that, but still I'm a ways from the time when things counted. The kick's gone—that's all."

"But you have interests, feelings, ambitions?"

"To make a living. I don't want to starve. There are pleasanter ways of dying."

When she did not answer and her gaze went from him he said, his eyes on her now, "That sounds pretty melodramatic, doesn't it? How in the world did we get so serious?"

"I'm a little tired of not being serious," Mrs Danby said.

"But here I am denying my own boast, talking about myself, boring you—not being gay."

"But why shouldn't you? I asked for it. And I'm not bored; I'm just puzzled. Once before you talked to me. Do you remember? Only it seems to me you were different then. You were not a man who sounded fed up with anything. You were interested, and you were interesting, and I liked it."

"I remember," said Faith.

"You talked about your flowers," said Mrs Danby quickly, "and you talked about your dogs. I remember they were beagles, weren't they?"

"They were beagles. Two of them."

"And the flowers. You said you grew zinnias. You said you liked them because they were jolly and they were hardy and they kept their chins up long after other flowers wilted—oh, I don't remember the exact words but that was the idea—and I remember you said you thought zinnias blossomed where the stars fell, or maybe it was the other way roundabout——"

"Sounds pretty mushy."

"No. It sounded like a man who wasn't afraid to be fond of something."

"The zinnias are still there," said Faith.

"But what has happened to you? Aren't you fond of them any more?"

Faith turned in his seat. "Listen," he said, and all his flippancy was gone, "I have feelings if I haven't ambition. Sure, I'm sentimental. I even recite poetry—don't worry, I won't. But here is the rub: nothing has happened to me! Oh, a dog dies; a friend dies; they happen to you, things like that. But the other things don't happen—the live things, the growing things, the things that make promises; they don't happen any more. Flowers aren't enough and they die too. So after a while you realize that it isn't going to happen, the coming of something to take the place of what you've lost; you realize that it isn't going to happen ever again, and you get a gone feeling inside you and you just quit chasing rainbows. See?"

Mrs Danby protested bravely. "Bosh! For a grown man I never heard such a crybaby! With all there is to love in the world, to live for—I don't mean moonlight and sunsets; I don't mean zinnias—I mean people, causes, friendships"——She stopped.

Faith said quietly, "Yes, you are right. And I suppose there is love. Things can still happen, can't they? You can happen!"

Mrs Danby did not answer. She was ridiculously aware of the beating of her heart and that something was impending for which she had not quite bargained. It recalled a tap on her shoulder, a voice urging her to put on a life belt.

"Dammit," said Faith huskily, "you're so swell to talk to!"

Mrs Danby looked up. Life belts could go hang. "Is that all I am?" she said, and her look and her question were so bare of coquetry they were almost impersonal. It was as if she asked herself—or kismet.

Faith took her hand.

"Listen, Mrs Gretchen Danby—Mrs Russell Danby—if ever I came to you; if I came to you in a month or a year or if I came to you tomorrow—if I said, 'I love you; will you go away with me?'—and if you knew what it meant, that it meant leaving all you have, breaking it up, throwing it away, swapping it for God knows what, maybe taking a chance on the very thing that was persuading you to go away, knowing that it might not be real, knowing that it might not last, but believing in it for the minute—would you go?"

You should have kissed me instead, she was thinking as she returned his gaze. The life belt was snugly on her now. And she smiled. And she shook her head.

"You must know," said Faith, "that I would never have you on any other terms."

Mrs Danby pushed his hand away lightly. She stepped from the car. In the moonlight she looked never more trim and alert and in the shadow of her hat he could fancy her accustomed friendly laugh.

"Good night, romantic Mr Faith," she said. "I really like you very much."

She was gone then and he sat unmoving while the steady flow of moonlight mocked him. When at last it occurred to him that the court of Greenfields was scarcely the appropriate place for the sun to wake him he tried to go easy with the starter and to slip as quietly as possible down the drive. Once he struck his knuckles to his temple and whispered, "You damn fool—you poor damn fool!"

Mrs Danby smoked her fifth cigarette. She continued to contemplate Rodney on the rug while hope lost to verity the little argument that the throbbing sound was a motor returning and not her own accusing pulse. When she rose from the couch and put out the cigarette her mind felt smirched. Rodney, she thought, will look like hell tomorrow. So will I. But tomorrow is another day. Things always seem different in the morning, don't they?

"My God, he's asleep," said the trooper on the ground.

"Already?" said the trooper at the wheel. "We wasn't two minutes behind him when he turned in."

"When he turned in? You mean the car turned in. It took them pasture bars like a horse going to hay."

"Gonna wake him?"

The trooper on the ground shook his head.

"I ain't got the heart. He looks too peaceful. But it beats me how he gets them tickets squared. We can't pull him now for drunken driving and if we take him for trespassing, I'll lay a bet him and Faith got a option on this field last week."

CHAPTER TWELVE
TOURISTS' REST

THEY were almost the last to leave the Inn. He was awkward about calling for his bill and the waitress had finished with the others by the time she caught his signal. When they rose from the table the waitress was already turning out the lights.

Selena took the lead across the dusky room, through the swinging screen and into the fanlight, and in a queer, sharp, hurting way he was acutely aware of the manner of her walk. Joe Purdy, who daily saw his mother brisk in yard and kitchen, who saw farm-women trudge the roads and the girls of Little Salem strolling, running like streaks, had never seen a woman walk before. So, in the taut, fantastic state of feeling brought on by the dogs and the melee and everything that had happened, she appeared to him, for though Selena Gillibo had often walked where he might watch, those times were not as now when, as she went before him, all of her moved upmost in his apperception.

At the top of the steps she waited. Across the highway the clock at Valley Service glowed like a fat illuminated pie, sliced at a quarter past twelve. While they watched, the long hand dropped another fraction.

"You've missed the bus," he said.

"Yes."

"That was my fault. I clean forgot, Selena. I never ought to acted the way I did, but it got me all upset and if it hadn't been for you—— Look, if you want me to drive you to New York——"

Selena shook her head. In her fixed attention to the clock she had become once more the woman of the store absorbed in some private enigma in which he had no part save as, perhaps, he might unwittingly provide a means. But when she turned, resting her full gaze on him, the throbbing in his chest redoubled.

"I don't know as I'm going to New York," Selena said.

He was startled by that; he was stumped to answer someone who, at midnight in the midst of loneliness, abandons an announced destination and who, if he took her look that way, looked to him for answer. But he remembered how, as they reached Madison, she had been vague and he seized on this reassurance that not he but her own will was responsible for a change of plan.

"You going back home then," he said rather than asked.

Still regarding him, she smiled, and now the paralysis to his thinking came from nothing but a simple thing, the sudden discovery of her eyes, how clear they were, how deeply dark yet clear and how soft in the smooth bell of her face. And he was shaken with the wish to prolong his nearness to her. To lose that nearness became intolerable; to delay that losing consumed him over doubt, worry, ardor, calculation.

"I'm not going back home," said Selena. "I'm not going back to Emil. I've quit Emil."

"You've quit Emil?"

She nodded calmly and, when he repeated the question in his same dull, disbelieving tone, impatiently caught his sleeve. The gesture made him again the schoolboy at her beck and call. "Come on—we better go."

But where—where, Selena?

The question followed him to the car, getting in, looking to see that the suitcase was safe, turning on the lights and waiting for another car to pass before he backed. They had gone, the merrymakers, the friends, the strangers; he and Selena were alone and that aloneness lit a flame beside which their earlier harmony was trivial. But mounting with elation came bewilderment, for Selena was not going home; she was not going to New York; she had quit her husband, Emil Gillibo, and what he was to do about it left him dumb and weaponless against the night.

As if she read him, "Drive west," Selena said and, when the highway ran before them, "There's places I can stop, places on the road"—a dike within her seemed to break—"it don't much matter where it is; I got money; I can get me a room; anywhere till I can catch a bus tomorrow. Maybe I won't go to New York; maybe I'll go to Easton or Trenton or Philadelphia; maybe I'll go farther away than that. That's all I want—to go!"

Catching her breath, she said, "I used to think it would be pretty awful to have no place to go. 'All dressed up and no place to go'—and now I don't care if I got no place to go; it 'll be better than where I been, where I been all my life and I got a lot of living left and I ain't going to spend it like that, I tell you, going on and on and on with nothing to do, nothing to look forward to——"

Her voice broke, but without a sob or whimper, and she spoke more slowly.

"You must know what I mean. You talked that way yourself. Only you're a man and you're young and you got it all ahead of you. Living, I mean, or whatever you want to call it. You can do something about it, can't you? Well, maybe it ain't too late for me either. It seems like I been asleep, like I been sort of trapped, but I woke up and I made up my mind it couldn't go on. I won't say nothing against Emil. Maybe it ain't exactly his fault and maybe I been pretty mean to him. But I can't help myself, the way I am either, and what's the use going on being mean to somebody and hating them and despising them when, if you got away, everything might be different?"

"For him too," she added, but immediately and violently, "Not that I care a snap! It don't matter to me what happens to Emil."

All this poured from her while he drove without a word, with his eyes on the road and no sign but the grim set of his face that he listened. They had passed Mike's Bar-B-Q and the turnoff to Little Salem and that light in the distance, she knew, was a place called Tourists' Rest. She did not know the people, who were new to that region, but maybe that was just as well and the cabins, they said, were clean and cost only a dollar.

"Look," she said, touching his arm, "I can stay there——Gee, Joe, I'm sorry; I wasn't thinking."

The car veered back to the concrete after its sudden lurch and he decreased their speed until they were opposite the fork. To their right a wooden arch spanned the way between two posts, from one of which a lantern hung. A hundred feet beyond another light glimmered in a house larger than the cabins receding among the trees.

"Well?" she said, for he remained at the wheel.

"I don't know as you ought to stay there."

"Why not?"

"I've heard it ain't decent."

Selena laughed. "Most any place's as good as another, I guess, and I never was a one to worry much about decency. I'll look after myself."

He glanced into the mirror; some way behind them headlights had topped the last hill. "I better turn off; there's a car coming."

But when he had passed the arch he still did not get out and it was Selena who opened her door and jumped to the ground.

"I wish," said Joe, "you wouldn't——"

She was in darkness where he looked across and down at her, yet that she smiled he felt sure and that to dissuade her was as hopeless as the misery in his heart. This is good-by, Selena. You will walk away from me into one of those dark little huts and tomorrow at sunup, or perhaps at about the time the team leads into the first furrow, you will be on your way, a woman I have known since childhood and not until this moment, when pain like a cut cries out against your going, cared shucks whether you lived or died.

Desperately he sought delay. "I'll bring your bag; you better find out first if they got room."

"All right," she said.

She left him then and he got out and lifted out her bag and listened to her footsteps fade and cease. The night drew in around him, full of loneliness and hush which not even that other car came on to break, and suddenly his pounding blood thinned to water. When Selena, returning a few minutes later, groped and touched his face it was wet.

"Why, Joe, what's the matter, honey?" she said.

She had entered the house and found a man, face stubbled and drawn for sleep, nodding in his shirtsleeves at a desk. She had asked him if he had a vacant cabin and, as she did so, laid down a dollar. The man, hauling himself to his feet, had looked at his ledger first and at her next, his eyes blinking redly behind thick lenses. "You alone, sister?" A foreboding prompted her to say that her husband was outside with the car, and when the man stonily took her dollar and handed her a key assigning her to Cabin 6 she had exulted at the smoothness of the lie. It was as easy, then, as that. But as she turned toward the door, "You forgot to register, sister," the man had said and she had halted, palpably dismayed. The man's gaunt face seemed to gloat. "Never mind, sister, but next time"—he was lowering himself into his chair— "next time it's gonna cost you two." In a rush of mortification that he thought her what so plainly he did she had fled without retort; her hand, reaching out to Joe, sought self-assurance more than his comfort.

Roughly he repulsed her. "Nothing's the matter! I got your bag. Where you want it put?"

"I'll take it," she said. He had been crying and didn't want her to know it, and this should have amused her but, oddly, she did not feel amused; she felt embarrassed and touched and, along with sympathy, suddenly lonely and anxious. But she said, scorning self-pity, "He had a cabin. It's number six. He said it was the last on the line," and when, as if he were in a hurry to end a situation, Joe picked up the bag and strode away she followed him with no word and no attempt to take the bag and a pang of gratitude for his protection which presently she would be without.

In the little time they had stood together the pitchy darkness had lightened. She glanced over her shoulder and saw the moon pushing through the treetops to the east. But here it was still black. She quickened her steps as she passed the cabins. No sound came from them and none from the motionless leaves overhead. It will be hot inside, she thought. Then a match flared and she came up to Joe before two wooden steps and a door with a numeral on it.

"This is it," he said.

He took the key and struck another match and unlocked the door and went in and, with a third match, found the switch. Light sprang harsh and dazzling. In its impact neither looked at the other but at the room, small, white painted, furnished with two cots, a dresser, table, chair. A smell of heat and pine and disinfectant pressed on them and Joe went to the single square window and raised the sash.

"It looks clean anyway," said Selena.

At the window he kept his back to her while one arm went up to his face, and she could imagine how he rubbed away the evidence of unmanning emotion. Whatever got into him, she wondered, and dismissed with a snub to her conceit the idea that anyone could be sad enough to see her go to cry. No, he was just a big kid who'd got the blues and then mad and then mopy from causes unakin to her and who, if he was acting kind of upset, was that way partly through shame that she had seen his weakness and partly through wishing for the moon and maybe out of awkward politeness. A sweet kid, she thought, yet more of a man than those other kids in Little Salem and more of a man than those other men, Harvey Slope and John Faith, and that man in that barroom that time and certain men who looked at her in a certain way when they met her on the streets of Madison. Joe was looking at her now, turned from the window, the light strong in his brown face and the blue eyes meeting hers, and if in his look she saw something of those others, she did not mind it in him, knowing that, for all his manhood, he was still just a big sweet kid. She smiled. "Well, Joe?"

He took a few steps toward her in one swift motion that brought him very near; he stopped as if with that nearness he had recovered something lost. His eyes implored her.

"Selena—I wish I was going with you! I don't want to go back home either. What I want isn't there any more. I don't know what I want but it ain't there. They can get along without me; most any fellow can do what I do for 'em and in a little while they wouldn't know the difference. You're going places where it won't matter what you say and what you think, and if you hit a spot you like you can stick there and make a place of your own. Home ain't my place. I don't know as it ever will be. I want to go away, Selena, and I don't want to go alone; I want to go with you!"

She heard him with her mind scarcely taking in what absurd thing he was proposing, for now the hunger in his eyes was suffusing her. She could only stare back in dumb acceptance of the bond that held them.

"Don't go!" Joe cried out suddenly.

Selena did not stir when he touched her. Not until his fingers had left her face, where they rested a moment as if to satisfy him that she was there; not until they crept on to the nape of her neck and down her back, clumsily, timidly, yet tightening to close the gap between them; not until that gap was closed and she was against him and his other hand pressed to her breast did she resist. Her hand took that other hand away.

"Don't," she whispered, "don't."

Joe let her go a little, a surrender of everything save her eyes still looking up and her shoulder, the last reality to be relinquished, but as she moved to loose even that he seized her and kissed her. Her hands went up, thrusting him off, while his lips, his arms imprisoned her, and then of a sudden she was thrusting no longer with her hands but with her body, ceding it completely and with the gift demanding and pursuing the return of his.

Emil watched them through the open door with no outward sign of emotion. He stood in the gravel a stride beyond the shaft of light, stooped a little, one knee a little bent, as a man might stand at rest after long labor. The gun stood with him, its butt on the ground, the barrel in his right hand. He did not know much about guns but he knew this was a twenty-gauge repeating shotgun and that, if a marksman stood close enough to the target, though how close was close enough, he could only guess, the charge would kill a man or—he added in his thought—a woman.

While he was waiting near the Inn he had considered the possibility that Selena might recognize the car. He had hesitated whether to park east or west of the Inn and decided on the east because if she were not coming back, and her clean sweep of the room above the store admitted of no doubt, she would go east to New York. If she saw the car—well, he would have to take a chance. The departure west caught him unprepared. In a ferment that the car would not start and then turning it frantically, he barely missed collision with the troopers and knew a moment's anguish that they would halt him while the quarry vanished. As it was, devils of uncertainty were racking him when he detected a distant light as it left the road. Not until he had parked a cautious way from Tourists' Rest and come up and spotted the Purdy Ford did a kind of relief ease him. He went back and got the gun. A light went on in the farthest cabin as he ducked from the road. Now he observed almost with apathy his wife in Joe Purdy's arms.

He was deadly tired. The suspicions and torments of the day, which had simmered and boiled and finally clotted into the single idea that he must save himself or revenge himself or in some masculine act of violence justify himself to himself, a reasoning no more clear in his head than the motives compounded of fear and shame and futile desire driving him on—all this muddle of suffering now sluggishly receded, leaving him as listless as a patient after fever. What he watched in the cabin, a concrete fact where all had been so hazy, brought him something like peace. Selena, guilty of God knew what plots and secrets, was indubitably guilty of this.

Suddenly he raised the gun, for the two inside had stepped back from their embrace. Emil crooked the gunstock in the hollow of his elbow and crawfished hastily.

Now, among the shadows and the trees, he could not be seen easily should one of them look out the door. But neither, he discovered, could he see so well, the lintel cutting off a quarter of his view. He began a stealthy withdrawal to the right. The window gave on that side of the cabin; if it was high yet not too high, he might see without risk of being seen.

He had gone a dozen yards, stopping a dozen times to listen for their voices, when two things happened: the broken murmur ceased and the door closed.

Emil, hugging the spot where he had frozen at that soft thud, stared at another spot bright ahead; then a third thing happened, and when he moved again he moved in utter darkness.

The window was high, higher than a tall man on tiptoe could reach, and so small that it would have seemed plausible for nothing, not even sound, to issue. Yet Emil, who could see only with his mind's eye, crouched there after sound had become less than the echo of a sigh. He began to shake. His hand gripped the gun barrel.

Joe came out of Kama, out of fervor and ecstasy and the little death, into blackness like a protecting cloak, soft and warm and luxurious, and in this velvet heart he lay torpidly while the fire tides seeped. The world stood still with time; he lay still with them. When, as if they would wrench him alert, small noises of the night insisted at his ears he clung to keep them out and learned, besides that ineffable other, comfort in Selena's answering caress. Thus, as the whispering started like wind stealing among foliage, it was but the night talking until a latch click stung him afoot.

"Whore!" the night shouted.

Joe flung himself at the ghost in the gray opening. As it came in to meet him his flying arm struck steel, and the night burst white in his face as once long ago a white burst had blinded him. He fell to his knees, clutching his eyes. When he opened them Selena had turned on the light and was staring down at Emil, whose head had been blown in at the right temple.

CHAPTER THIRTEEN
ROUTE 28

THIS NIGHT of July Fourth, with the sky cloudless and the moon full above the Valley, was such a perfect summer's night as might solace the most anxious heart. Yet, as John Faith rolled into its radiance down Mrs Danby's drive, its beauty and its peace only enhanced the sickness that had fallen upon him. Pulling off the highway, he stopped his car. The Musconetcong Range communed with heaven; somberly he regarded both.

John Faith was forty-seven years old. For thirty-five years, from the time he sold papers on the streets of his native city, he had worked in many occupations, none of which brought him wealth. In his work, in eating, drinking, sleeping, he had consumed four fifths of his days on earth. He had experienced passion, friendship, much joy, some sorrow; he had found a little time to think. His faith in God he had lost early, substituting for it a belief in life. This had been sufficient until, first from his own life and then from the lives of others where they touched his, a quality began to go. His notice of this fact was gradual, like that of a man gradually growing deaf who one day becomes inattentive, next is asking for things to be repeated and at last does not hear at all. John Faith's spirit—if that was the appropriate word—had gone deaf; for some time, when life spoke, he had but pretended to listen.

But tonight he had heard a voice, singing through that wall of pretense and indifference to wake in him a strange emotion. It was elation and it was veneration and it was desire and he had greeted it with eagerness and yet with fear. He had forgotten such a thing might be. If it was real, he must hold it preciously; if it was not ...

"But most evidently it was not," he said aloud. "The lady was amused. And you, romantic Mr Faith, are a fool. There was a time to build up and a time to love, but these are the days of darkness."

Yet I suppose, he brooded, I should consider myself fortunate. I belong to one of the few lands left on earth where men are still free to pursue happiness. In this small corner of northern New Jersey hope and courage are as common as apples. The young and the old, the haves and the have-nots, the Trimbles and Havlas, the Gillibos and Gundersons and Purdys, they are clinging desperately to life though it turns on them and tears them, and not one but looks forward to tomorrow with belief implicit in his chance of victory. Only I, who once found hope and courage here, no longer possess a damn's worth of either.

"It is a time to cast away," he informed the hills. "Your time and other people's time—so short yet such a lot when it's all as empty as last night's pint. So you blindly kill other people's time, and when someone says, 'I'll help kill yours,' you run like a coward. But that's where your damn feelings interfere. If you still have them or what's left of them you hug them, don't you? Oh no, you can't risk gambling your last feeling, if it's only the capacity to suffer. And you don't gamble with someone else's feelings, do you? That's not cricket, as the goddamn British say. You can kill other people's time but not their feelings. So what can you do? Well, you can get drunk."

Very well, Faith—said Faith to himself—you will now get drunk. You will cross the county, if necessary, to find a bottle; you will drink yourself groggy; you will spout boozy, sentimental poetry as meaningless as your life, and at length you will zigzag into some friendly meadow where the weary are at rest. Let's to the daisies, Jack!

With that Faith released his brake.

He had reached, on Route 28, an intersection where the road to the left would take him to Frank's place, which never closed as long as one drink remained outside a customer, and where the road to the right passed Jerry's, of similar name, when he saw the car coming. It was coming fast from the west on 28 and Faith, an old hand at country driving, decided he had better duck. He turned; if he himself was still a little drunk, the shock to his bumpers more than sobered him.

He got out, sore—in mind and stomach—where the wheel had dug. The other car was in the ditch. He looked at his own first, saw the damage was nothing that a good mechanic could not straighten and, limping designedly, approached the wreck. With some satisfaction he perceived a front wheel hopelessly twisted.

"Serves you right, friend. When a guy gives you the signal—— Well, I'm damned!"

Joe Purdy's frightened face cheered him into such a grin as he had not enjoyed in months.

"It's young Lochinvar! What's the hurry, boy? Was Emil after you? I beg your pardon, Mrs Gillibo!"

They got out. They did not limp; they did not grin. In the revealing moonlight they stood, Joe a little ahead of the woman, as if the accident had struck them speechless.

"Well, now, I'm sorry," said John Faith. "Maybe it was my fault. It looks like I busted up something. It looks like I busted up your car, for one thing. Don't worry—I'll get her fixed. Are you folks okay?"

"Emil's dead, Mr Faith!" Joe Purdy burst out.

Faith stopped in his stride. From his gaunt height his head cocked inquiringly toward that incredible word.

"Dead?"

"He musta followed us. I don't know how it happened. The gun went off. I didn't even know it was him——"

Selena caught his arm. "Don't tell him, Joe!"

So she was not frightened. She was tense; she was defiant, but she was not frightened. Faith slowly put his hands in his pockets.

"Well, now, Mrs Gillibo, I think maybe he better had. If Emil got shot by a gun, I think maybe he better tell me all about it."

She did not take her eyes from him. Her look said: I know you; you are John Faith, who helps people in trouble; but you have never helped me, John Faith; you were too shrewd and I did not trust you; nor do I know that I should trust you now.

Faith said, "To begin with, Mrs Gillibo, are you sure he's dead? If a fellow just got shot and you rushed off for the doctor——"

"He's dead all right," she said.

Joe Purdy broke in. "We weren't going for any doctor! And he's dead, Mr Faith! It blew his head off!"

"Oh," said Faith. "I see," he said. But because he did not see he did not go on and Joe could not endure his silence.

"We was there—the two of us—and the room was dark when he come in. He come in yelling and I didn't know who it was——"

"You better let me tell him, Joe," said Selena, "if you got to tell him."

Her eyes on Faith no longer defied him; they asked him simply to believe her.

"It wasn't his fault," she said. "None of it. Joe's, I mean. I asked him to take me to the bus, and when we missed it he rode me just to help me out. That was why he was there. He'd carried my bag in. That was all——"

"Selena!"

"You let me do the talking," she said and took Joe's hand and held it close in front of her. "It don't matter what Emil thought. He was wrong. I guess he was watching; I wouldn't put it past him; you ought to know how he was. Well, when the light went out——"

She hesitated briefly.

"They do, you know, most everywhere. They do in the store a lot, sometimes when they're working on the line and sometimes it's trouble at the plant. Anyway, if he was watching and saw it go out he musta thought something and he come in yelling, like Joe said. Of course Joe went for him and Emil had a shotgun and someway it went off. He was killed all right. But it wasn't Joe's fault. Ain't that about the way it was, Joe?"

To that level gaze Joe Purdy made no answer but the desperation of his own. Their eyes and hands stayed fast and John Faith rubbed his chin.

"Well, now," he said, "well, now. I knew Emil was jealous but I didn't know he was that big a fool. Did he ever talk of suicide, Mrs Gillibo?"

"He'd never have done that," she said.

"But you can't tell. Nobody can tell. Was a fellow over by Norton once committed suicide. Nobody thought he'd ever have the guts. But he did. Shot himself with a shotgun too. Got barefoot and put the barrel in his mouth and pulled the trigger with his toe. I don't suppose Emil was barefoot, was he?"

Selena, watching him, shook her head.

"No? That's too bad. But you can't tell about that either. It might be done with the heel of a shoe. Did anybody hear the shot? It would take more than a shot, I guess, to wake the old man."

Selena shook her head again. The hope in her stare had died.

"You don't understand," she said. "Emil didn't get killed at home."

"No?" said Faith. "I don't understand. Where did he get killed?"

"In a cabin at Tourists' Rest."

All three were silent then, the two with locked hands waiting for him, looking to him for solution, and John Faith looked away, into the moonlight, into the hills.

"That's bad," he said. "I'm afraid that's very bad. But let me think a minute. You've got to tell me, you know; you've got to tell me the truth. You two took a cabin at Tourists' Rest?"

"No," said Selena. "I took the cabin. I was going away. I was quitting Emil. That was as far as I got. I had to stay somewhere."

"Did he know it, that you were quitting him?"

"I guess he did. He came home just before we left. He must have seen us go."

"And trailed you with the gun. The poor, doggoned fool! Who saw you at Tourists' Rest?"

"The man. The man who runs the place. At least, he saw me."

Faith said sharply, "Just how do you mean?"

"I mean he couldn't have seen Joe. Joe waited outside with the bag. He asked me if I was alone and I said my husband was with me——"

She stopped and in her glance toward Joe was a distress that Faith had never seen in her before. He doubted that any man had seen it.

"I had to tell him that, Joe," she said. "I was afraid he wouldn't give me the cabin if I said I was alone. It didn't mean nothing bad. You know that, don't you?"

Faith spoke roughly, trying to be cool. "Look here, we're losing time. That fellow must have heard the shot. Did he see you afterward? Did he see you leave?"

Selena said, "I don't know. We hurried. I made Joe go. It wasn't Joe's fault!"

"But yes it was, Selena! It was as much my fault as yours. I wanted you; I——"

"Skip it," snapped Faith. "The troopers may be there by now; we've got to step on it."

He stood pondering them like a judge, and they waited with the submission of the defenseless.

At last he said, and his voice was not ungentle, "I'm afraid you're hooked, Selena. Any way it breaks you're hooked. As soon as they identify Emil they'll look for you and that fellow will describe you and they'll figure the rest. Couple stops at tourist camp—husband surprises them—bang! No, it won't look sweet; it won't be easy to prove self-defense; it will look to any jury just about the way it will look to them."

Suddenly he clapped a fist into a palm.

"But there's one thing they don't know; there's one thing they haven't got! They haven't got the man!"

He addressed Joe directly, speaking so imperatively that immediately he was out of all keeping with the John Faith Joe knew, that Mr Faith who still kidded when he was serious, that Mr Faith you must always take with a grain of salt. This was a man in deadly earnest and a man you must obey unquestioningly.

"Joe, listen carefully. Do what I tell you to do if it's the hardest thing you ever did in your life. What's right and what's wrong doesn't matter now. Emil's dead. We can't bring him back. You didn't kill him; Selena didn't kill him; he didn't kill himself. But the law won't accept that. The law's bound to make somebody suffer, and if you suffer you won't suffer alone. Your mother's going to suffer and your father and everything that might mean something to you someday. But nobody has to suffer if you keep your mouth shut. You understand? Keep it shut! Keep it shut no matter what happens. I'm taking Selena with me. She's got a chance to get away. It's just a chance. Don't let your conscience hurt you. Mine won't. What the hell? It wasn't her fault any more than it was yours. It was just one of those things. Now beat it! Go by the back roads; go by the fields. Leave the car where it is and if anybody asks you about it, a hit-and-runner smashed you. They'll guess it was the killer. There's just one thing. Where's the gun? Was it Emil's gun?"

Selena answered. "He never owned a gun. I don't know where he got it. It's there, in Joe's car. I picked it up. I don't know why——"

"The female of the species, eh? This goes deeper than I thought. You probably made a mistake. But never mind. Get the gun, please. Put it in my car. I hope to God she can still travel."

As Selena walked quickly away Faith gripped Joe's shoulder, looking down at him hard, looking a little as he had looked only a few hours before, when they stood together in the hot shadows of Trimble's lane.

"You understand? You'll do what I say?"

"Yes, Mr Faith."

"And you'll never tell a soul, no matter what happens?"

"Yes sir."

"Okay, boy. You've got a lot to live for, Joe. Chance did you a dirty trick tonight. Don't let it lick you."

"But what about you, sir?"

"Never mind about me. If you ever feel you owe me anything, there's a way you can square it. Be kind to the land. Maybe I'll explain what I mean someday."

"But Selena—I can't run off and leave her!"

"You're not running off. The worst thing you can do for her is to stick. Better beat it before she comes back."

He gave the shoulder a hard push, and when Selena, returning, reached his side Joe was a shadow among the willows.

At the brook he turned and Selena's hand went up. But Faith caught it.

"Don't, Mrs Gillibo. It won't be easy for him. You're not going to make it harder, are you?"

She faced him then, removing her hand but not her eyes from his, and what he saw dismayed him for the outcome of his plan.

A long way off the Musconetcongs echoed a motorcycle's stutter.

Beyond the brook the fields stopped at barbed wire, and beyond the barbed wire the woods began, ascending to the very top of the Barrens. Joe Purdy came through the woods into a dirt road spattered with moonlight. He came running, panting, not slowing his steps for the rising ground, for something had happened to him back there; something had gobbled among the trees and reached fingers through the dark to chill the back of his neck, and it was Emil and it was the Law and it was Death and Fear. He had run with no more power to control himself than a soul fleeing the devil.

Now he dropped into a trot and soon to a walk, for he knew the road. He could see it in his mind for two miles ahead, each curve and hummock that brought him nearer and, at last, the break in the woods through which he could look across at his own fields and his own barns and the tin roof white above the room where each morning he opened his eyes to dawn, tracing on the ceiling the crack that was like a river on a map. Suddenly he stopped.

He was running home. He was running home as instinctively as a helpless kid who has cut his finger or been bullied by the older boys. He was running home because nowhere else could he escape the thing at his heels. But in escape he was forfeiting a possession he might never again recover: pride. The woman who had filled him, the tragedy he had brought on her, the friend who had saved him—he was abandoning obligation and honor in a panic. Contempt for his cowardice bore into him with the force of a blow.

Down there on the road, as he listened, caught on the point of his gaze, to Mr Faith's commands, flight had seemed not only the right but the one thing left to do. Now doubt sickened him and shame defeated fear. He took a step backward, stumbled and steadied himself against the bank. He must go back. And in the instant of decision came a flash of futility. Go back to what? A wreck by an empty roadside? Mr Faith would be gone; Selena would be gone, and where they went he did not know; he would be alone against terror.

A sense of loss shot through him with a pang that was all but physical. Selena! The warm earth cried her name. He put his arms against the bank and cried as he had not cried since childhood.

"Get in," said Faith. "Seconds may make a lot of difference."

She wheeled from those serene, forbidding hills.

"I've got to get away! You don't know what it means!"

"I can guess."

"No—you don't know. I never loved Emil; I hated him. I'm glad he's dead!"

He said nothing, urging her with a gesture, and when he was beside her in the car—Selena clenching and unclenching her hands, agitated as he had never believed she could be—he stayed grimly silent.

"I'd-a made a good wife if things had been different! Even a farmer's wife! I never felt that way till tonight but I do now! The store, the country, being poor—that wasn't everything——"

He drove his foot down and, as the generator whirred without effect, sweat wet his forehead.

"I've got to get away!" she repeated.

"Yes," he said, "yes, I know."

He tried again.

"And if I do," she said, "you've got to tell Joe where I am!"

Faith eased his efforts. His bloodshot eyes glared.

"Forget it, Mrs Gillibo. You can't do that."

"Oh yeah?" she retorted fiercely. "It's easy for you to say. But you don't know. We was going away! Going away together! He said he wanted to! He——"

Gas caught and held. The motor roared.

"Let's go," said Faith.

They were doing sixty coming out of Madison. The highway wound circuitously, but Faith kept his speed. Tires screeched on curves; the needle leaped on the straightaways. Selena sat taut.

At a bridge over the Raritan they slowed. The shotgun splashed in midstream.

"That's that," said Faith. "They'll never find it there."

She made no answer. Tight-lipped, she watched the road.

"That was Joe's gun," said Faith, lifting his voice against the wind. "Did you know that?"

She shook her head.

"I've handled it a many a time," he shouted. "If they'd got it, it would have been too bad."

He heard Selena dimly.

"Joe never killed him! He as good as killed himself!"

"Oh, I believe you! But how will it look to the cops? It won't look bad without the gun. Not for Joe. If they catch you, Mrs Gillibo, the man they catch you with is the man Emil caught you with!"

He heard her gasp. She said something.

"What?" he cried. They were going up a long hill into construction flares. Faith did not hesitate. In a whirl of dust they missed the concrete and regained it. The flares died like matches in a wind.

"Why are you doing this?" she demanded.

"We've got to, Mrs Gillibo. If we can make Somerville okay we'll hit the back roads."

"I don't mean speeding. Why did you make Joe go?"

"Oh—that, Mrs Gillibo. I'll tell you someday, when I know."

A truck crawled on a grade and Faith passed it at the crest. The little towns loomed—Anandale, Lebanon, White House—and those dark homes and quiet shrubs they left in the same flash that revealed them.

"You can't take Joe away from me!" she cried suddenly. "You can't take me away from him!"

"Listen—you!" he flung from the side of his mouth. "Do you think I like doing this?"

"Why do you do it then?"

"God knows. It's an old habit."

"Then let's go back. They'll believe me like you did!"

"Don't be a damn fool. They'll give you twenty years and maybe Joe the chair."

"I'll tell them I did it! I'll tell them what Emil was like! They'll believe me! They'll let me go!"

"You're crazy, Mrs Gillibo—is that one light or two behind us?"

In the black mirror a star grew to a moon and above the roar she heard the siren.

"It's them!" she cried and in her voice he heard, with anger, a sob of relief. "We might as well give up!"

"Oh no we won't. That's Somerville ahead."

Then, as they roared over a rise, he saw the second moon.

"They've got us, Mrs Gillibo—coming and going. But there's one way out if you really give a damn for Joe. The man they catch you with is the man Emil caught you with, alive or dead. Are you game, Mrs Gillibo?"

In his eyes, as he turned from the shaking wheel, she read his wild intention.

"No!" she cried. "No!"

An automobile going seventy-five miles an hour down a steep incline can jump a road from a slight impulse. It might have been Selena's hand on Faith's arm that unbalanced the scales. The troopers never knew. When they skidded to a halt after the detonation the big tree was severed as if a shell had hit it and flames were already bright on contorted metal.

Joe lifted his face from his arms. He brushed away soil. When he went on he was dry eyed, depleted of emotion. But as he walked, to the tired muscles blood returned and vigor to the exhausted mind and heart and he could look ahead with something that was hard and stoical forming over the softness and the dread. The moon was down a little. In another hour the east would be gray. Birds would begin to twitter and where he walked the young rabbits would appear. Life, stirring in the woods and fields, would stir on the cleared lands, on the farms; smoke would rise and stock wake and the long day call.

www.ingramcontent.com/pod-product-compliance
Lightning Source LLC
Chambersburg PA
CBHW020312260626
47156CB00016B/2786